THE GYPSY CHRONICLES

*When The Mind Goes
All That's Left to Use is the Body*

ARTOOLLIOUS

Copyright © 2018 Artoollious
All rights reserved
First Edition

NEWMAN SPRINGS PUBLISHING
320 Broad Street
Red Bank, NJ 07701

First originally published by Newman Springs Publishing 2018

ISBN 978-1-64096-534-8 (Paperback)
ISBN 978-1-64096-535-5 (Digital)

Printed in the United States of America

PART I

1

The Gypsy spent the last part of his life wandering. He tried to adjust back to "normal" life (whatever that was supposed to mean). He still had his looks, his strength, and "those" eyes. They were called that on more than one occasion. Even though his mind and body were beaten and bruised by the wars that he served in, he still had "those" eyes. He knew how to use them as well (that thought always made him smile).

His eyes were the color of the Caribbean Sea with flecks of slate and teal. They were ever so slightly cocked in his head as to always look just a little sad. That was something that always seemed to work in his favor. They were perfectly covered by long lashes and, the only other hair on his head, his chestnut eyebrows, which were beginning to show some streaks of gray.

He always had a touch of a belly for someone so fit; even so, that never bothered him. The only thing about his looks he ever disliked was his nose. He always thought the end looked oddly bulbous.

Vanity, he mused as he kicked a can down the road. *What a waste of time.*

His back was beginning to hurt. He would have to find a place to stop for the night and take his "meds." Luckily he was near a town that looked like his type of place. Of course, he fit in in a lot of places—most, in fact. This town would turn out to be a little different, and his undoing.

The Gypsy slid into the country and western bar just off the highway he walked down. Rachael's was the name—named after the owner, he was sure.

He did not care for the new style of country music that played on the jukebox when he walked in, though. To him it all just sounded like hip-hop with an accent. Give him Hank Jr., Waylon, Willie, and the boys. Johnny, Kris, and all the other bandits always suited his lifestyle anyway. What was it the Bellamy Brothers sang?

> He's an old hippie
> and he don't know what to do.
> Should he hang on to the old?
> Should he grab on to the new?

Hmm, he thought as he scanned the room. *Sage words.*

He found a slightly lit corner at the bar where he could sit and scout out prospective customers and, of course, where he could *be* seen. His injuries did not prevent him from earning a living, but the only living he was able to figure out how to get his broken mind and body to perform was the "oldest profession," and it was not exactly legal anywhere except in Vegas.

And they can keep it! he thought with a slight chuckle.

The Gypsy never cared for all the glitz and lights. He always preferred a simple way. The desert. Or the mountains. Or the woods. The fewer people, the better. Which was really a pity since he really relied on them to make a living. Yet another one of life's little twists that always made him chuckle.

The chain-smoking bartender strolled over as he sat down at the bar. She was a bleach-bottle blond in her (maybe) midsixties. She was definitely damaged goods from an abusive relationship who knew how to work a smile and a wink for a tip just like the Gypsy did. She wore jeans that should have been reserved for her granddaughter, but even with those slight bulges in the wrong places, she made you want to take them off of her and relieve them both of the stresses they showed.

She had the jeans paired with a nice red-and-black flannel shirt and black suspenders. The shirt was unbuttoned just enough so that one was able to see her tan line and just enough of the cleavage to know what she was packing, but not so much as to start a fight. The suspenders were used to frame her *assets* properly. The whole ensemble was accessorized with a cowboy hat, belt, buckle, and boots that had all seen very many miles just like their owner, but still appeared to have been well loved and appreciated.

"What'll ya' have, Blue-Eyes?" she asked with the raspy chain-smoker's voice as she batted her eyes playfully at the Gypsy.

He almost took the bait but thought better of it. "Just a beer and a bag of peanuts, love," he said with a smile and a wink.

As she walked away, the Gypsy thought, *If no other prospects present themselves... Maybe.*

If she were fifteen or twenty years younger and *not* damaged goods... *Definitely*, he thought with a slight smirk and chuckle.

The Gypsy swung the barstool around to survey the room and see if anyone might be in need of his services. He was not surprised to find that there was a young strawberry-blond that eyed him. She was leggy in skin-tight jeans that rode pleasingly low in the front. She wore an oddly checkered flannel shirt twisted up in front between her perfectly round, slightly larger-than-a-softball breasts. The shirt was made in psychedelic colors and looked as if the stripes were melting. It almost made the Gypsy wish he had some acid. She had those skin-tight jeans tucked into some custom ostrich-skin boots. Those boots must have cost *someone* a bundle. They had very pointed toes covered with what looked to be heavily engraved, gold-plated tips. The tops were floppy and had both outside and rear pulls. The pulls had gold embellishments depicting Bengal tigers engraved on them.

As this "little kitten" two-stepped her way to the latest hip-hop/country song over to where the Gypsy warmed up his smile, he tried to decide if she were a prospective customer or a professional herself.

"Buy me a drink, Blue-Eyes?" Kitten asked.

"Maybe latter, Kitten," the Gypsy coyly replied with a slightly crooked, smirky smile and an ever-so-slight wink. "I'm working right now." His smile grew slightly and turned into an ever-so-slight pucker. The pucker was so small it might not even have been seen in the low light.

To the Gypsy's delight, Kitten's eyes sparkled. She glanced around and then leaned in and asked, "How much?"

2

The Gypsy arrived back at the bar an hour and a half later with five hundred dollars and the memories of a *very* flexible and athletic young kitten, and a couple of new scratches to boot. The kitten was a lot of fun. Clients like her were the ones he liked the best. The free spirits. He always hated the "cheaters," the unhappy ones—especially when they were men. They were always the worst. No wonder their wives hated them and would not have sex with them. Blah, blah, blah… It was the same story every time.

Dude! Wake up. Divorce her and go find a man. You're obviously gay! Go be happy and stop making everyone around you miserable, the Gypsy thought. He just shook his head and chuckled.

When he walked into the bar, he saw a nice, clean-shaven young man at the opposite end of the room who definitely looked out of place. Most of the patrons were sweaty, beer-swilling, dirty jean–wearing biker, trucker, or cowpoke types. They all needed a shave and a haircut. Not that there was anything wrong with those types. The Gypsy spent some time with people like them before. He enjoyed those times immensely. He might have even loved a couple of them if the situations turned out differently.

But this "kid" stood out like a bad haircut on school picture day. To call him a "Twink" would have been an understatement. If he was in a town with a strong ice-skating culture, and if he possessed the talent, he would have made a fine figure skater. The Gypsy could easily imagine him in a skin-tight unitard covered in sequins.

At least the Twink wore jeans and cowboy boots. Unfortunately, they were pressed and polished to within an inch of their lives. He wore a button-up dress shirt buttoned *all* the way up. It was pressed as well as his jeans were.

They both probably stood up on their own from all the starch, the Gypsy thought as he watched the Twink try to walk like he "had a pair." That thought made him laugh out loud a little.

The Twink was thin but not too thin. His jeans fit nicely around the seat and held well as he walked. In the front, they were not too tight as to be uncomfortable but were pleasing to watch no matter what direction he moved. The shirt just fit enough so you could see his physique, letting you know that he did not exercise much, if ever, but he was still pleasingly fit-looking. His hair was dark—very dark, but not black. In this light it looked almost dark magenta. The Gypsy thought maybe he had a bad dye job that was growing back out. His hair hung just past shoulder-length. It was parted down the middle and flowed with every move and breeze. It was not straight or curly, but a little in between. It looked natural, not like a perm.

Yes, he was pretty.

And he did not belong here. Every time someone walked in, he tried to smile at them to initiate some form of human contact. That was when the Gypsy noticed a couple of bikers. They eyed the Twink in a way that usually led to trouble so he decided to intervene.

"Hi," the Gypsy said with a seductive smile after he approached the Twink. "Let's get out of here."

The Twink looked surprised and started to hesitate, but the Gypsy interrupted him, "I'll explain outside."

When they were outside, the Gypsy explained what he saw. The Twink thanked him. They struck up a friendly conversation as they walked toward the parking lot around back of the bar where the Twink said his car was parked.

"You really shouldn't be in this bar, kiddo," the Gypsy started. "Those animals will kill you."

"*Rachael's* is the only place in *this* town I have to go," the Twink replied.

"Then leave," the Gypsy stated flatly. "Believe me when I tell you, if you stay here, you will die here… soon."

The Twink looked scared but understood the reality that there was nothing here for him. He looked up into the Gypsy's deep blue eyes that looked back down at him with kindness. The Twink wondered if he should lean up and kiss him. Before he got the chance, the Gypsy said, "Let's go back to your place and talk about what you need to do and go from there."

Those words had a soothing effect on the Twink, and he said, "Yes."

The Gypsy opened the Twink's door to his convertible BMW 4 series so he could get in and then politely shut it behind him. The Gypsy walked around the champagne-colored (of course it was) ragtop that was cleaned and pressed to within an inch of its life just like the Twink's clothing. As he started to open the door and get in, he noticed the bartender. As she emptied some trash, she watched him leave again with another "client." She gave him a coy smile, a wink, and a nod.

The barmaid could not help but notice how the Gypsy was dressed now that they were outside in better light. She always hated how low light was in the bar and wanted to change it. But she never seemed to find the time to do it. He had on a nice dress shirt that she thought was probably silk. It was long-sleeved with a pattern in dark magenta tones—not quite paisley but some '60s psychedelic pattern, just minus the wild colors. It accented his dark, tanned skin well. He had on some cowboy boots that accentuated his height. The Gypsy had broad but not too broad shoulders, and Rachael wanted to grab them and pull him down onto her.

The Gypsy smiled and winked back as he got in the Twink's car and thought, *Damn it. I may have to give out ANOTHER freebie.*

So that's the job I overheard him tell that rich slut Chasity Monroe he's workin' *at,* the barmaid thought while she watched him *escort* another one out of *her* bar as she emptied the trash. *I'm gonna have to give him something to work on after the bar closes. He needs to work off some of that damn rent!* she thought with a huff as she hoisted the second can and dumped it into the dumpster.

3

The Gypsy was surprised by how close the Twink lived to the bar to have driven. Only two blocks.

This younger generation, he thought.

The Twink parked the car in the garage, and they walked up to his loft. It was nicely decorated in an industrial/Victorian style. Not quite steampunk. A little more Broadway than that, but well done and not gaudy.

They went over to the kitchenette, and the Twink got a bottle of Veuve Clicquot La Grande Dame and poured a couple of glasses. Champagne. Of course, it was champagne. With the Twink's style, he would not have anything to drink but champagne. The Gypsy never cared for the stuff. He did not want to be rude, so he took a sip after the customary clink of the glasses. *Wow*, he thought. *This is better than the stuff I've tried before. I'd still rather have a pint of bitter any day.*

After a cursory glance over the Twink's apartment, the Gypsy asked if he could take his "meds." The Twink asked what he meant, and the Gypsy produced a small black leather sachet with a small vial of a white powder, a syringe, foldable spoon, and flip-top lighter engraved in a red, white, and blue lacquered "USA" with the American flag and bald eagle. The Twink nodded yes. After the Gypsy got set up, the Twink asked if he could try some. The Gypsy explained why he used this "medication" and that if it were not for his injuries, he would not use it.

The Gypsy said, "If you do not have to take it, don't. Once you start down this road, it's a hard one to get off of."

The Twink seemed like he understood, but to drive his point home, the Gypsy added, "And you don't *need* it."

While they sat on the edge of the bed, the Twink looked up at the Gypsy and smiled. From where they sat, the Gypsy noticed how the bed was positioned to give the best view out the window.

How romantic, he thought.

He was sure it was intentional by whoever decorated. After he finished taking his "meds," he placed his arm around the Twink and pulled him close while the pain subsided.

They talked a long time while they sat on the end of the bed. The Twink was still just a child in many ways even though he was legally an adult. He most likely just turned twenty-one. He needed to leave this town and grow. The Gypsy traveled more than most had dreamed. He met a great many people during his travels. Some of them were people the Twink could stay with and fit in perfectly.

"I know some people in Vegas you could stay with. They are really good people and can be trusted to tell you whom you can trust," the Gypsy started as the Twink looked up at him with interest.

"They're in show business. They're drag queens, and the only reason I stayed as long as I did in that place. They are *all* good people and will not steer you wrong. Except maybe Lacie. Watch out for Lacie. She's a little wild. She likes the nose candy just a 'little' too much," the Gypsy had to stop and chuckle for a second at some of those memories.

As the Gypsy paused, the Twink took the opportunity to interject a comment. "If you think it would be the place for me, then I'll go. Can I ask you something?"

"Sure," he replied.

"Will you come with me?"

After an ever-so-brief pause, he answered with a kind smile, "No. This is an adventure of growth you need to make on your own. We may meet again sometime in the future."

The Gypsy leaned in and kissed the Twink more passionately than he was ever kissed before.

The Gypsy stopped with the kiss. The Twink looked up at him. He was confused. He longed for more. He was ready for the Gypsy to be his first. The Gypsy held his hand up to his lips. He stopped the Twink from continuing. He knew from experience that this child was not ready.

The Gypsy gently caressed the Twink's cheek. He brushed back his hair and said, calmly and soothingly, "Wait. *Your* first time needs to be with someone very special. Intimate. You'll know when the time is right. Don't rush it. It's worth the wait," he paused briefly between each sentence to accentuate his point.

The Twink fell into him and wrapped his arms around him as tightly as he was able. They sat that way for a great time. After the Twink released his grip on the Gypsy, the Gypsy asked, "Would you like me to help you get packed?"

"Yes," he replied shyly with those cute doll eyes. "I don't have much to pack," which did look to be true. But what he did have appeared to be very nice.

The Gypsy and the Twink packed the Twink's few possessions from the large space. They talked about his possible future and talked about nothing at all.

Around four in the morning, when the Gypsy knew was the best time to catch Che'tanai (pronounced she-tah-nā, followed with a snap—always followed with a snap), he placed the call. Che'tanai was a tall, leggy black man of forty with all the youth, exuberance, and attitude of an eighteen-year-old girl. He always reminded the Gypsy of RuPaul just a little. Maybe that was whom Che was trying to emulate.

Che answered the phone with his usual "What's up, girl?"

The Gypsy explained to Che'tanai the Twink's situation. As he knew Che would, Che accepted the Gypsy's idea for the Twink to stay with him, and he invited the Twink to come to Vegas straight away.

After they finished packing his bimmer, the Twink and the Gypsy looked over the loft one last time.

The Twink said to the Gypsy, "This place is paid for until the end of the month. If you like, I can arrange for you to stay here until the lease runs out."

The Gypsy thought about if for a second, but it was far too nice and just not his style. He replied, "While a *very* generous offer, I have to decline. It's just not my style. I would *not* be comfortable here."

He smiled and gently brushed back that dark mane away from those innocent eyes. Those sweet doe eyes. If he weren't...

They got back to the bar about 4:30 a.m. As the Gypsy got out of the Twink's car, he noticed the barmaid stood in the same spot with the same shit-eatin' grin on her face that she wore when they left.

Had she even moved? he thought as he walked around to the driver's side of the car to say his final farewell to the Twink.

As the Gypsy stood there and bid farewell to the Twink, the barmaid took the opportunity to admire his ass. The jeans he had on fit just right. The waist was not too high, nor were they hip-hugger jeans. They were right in the middle. And Rachael wanted them wadded up in the middle of the barroom floor. He was driving her crazy! The Gypsy shifted his weight from one foot to the other foot slowly. This allowed each gluteal muscle to slowly and separately flex and relax.

That bastard has to be doing that on purpose, Rachael thought.

"Be careful," the Gypsy said as he touched the Twink's hand while it rested on the top of the door. "You should get to Vegas before noon. Che's place is easy to find."

"Are you sure you won't come with me?" the Twink asked. "I'll miss you."

The Gypsy smiled and then bent down and kissed the top of the Twink's head after he brushed his hair back one last time.

The barmaid watched as the Gypsy bent over to say goodbye.

Did he actually bow his legs a little so I would be able to check out his package? she thought in a near-rage.

With that final kiss, the Twink knew it was time to leave, so he smiled and waved goodbye as he pulled away to start a new life.

The Gypsy needed to remember to call Che. He needed to make sure he understood this one was special. The Twink was not like the others the Gypsy sent his way before. And to make *damn* sure Lacie stayed the hell away from him. That crazy crack whore would eat the Twink alive.

I guess there's always something to be concerned with, the Gypsy thought as he watched the taillights fade down the end of the street.

4

The Gypsy slowly spun around. He looked at the barmaid as she stood next to the dumpster. She still had a shit-eatin' grin proudly displayed on her face.

What's her game? he wondered. *Is this her idea of flirting?*

He said nothing as he approached her and just shot her a crooked smirk and sideways glance as if to say, "Okay, what of it?" He tossed his duffel bag down at her feet, picked up the full trash can next to her that still needed to be emptied and, without ever breaking their gaze, placed its contents within the waste receptacle. He then retrieved his duffel and followed her back inside where she offered him a drink.

"How 'bout some Crown, Blue-Eyes?"

"Since *you're* buying, sure," he replied.

She poured them both a large shot and then held up her glass for the customary toast.

"To your health," he said.

The barmaid leaned in close, stared the Gypsy directly in "those eyes," and said, "To good times."

After they both threw back their shots, the barmaid threw her glass across the room. She leaped across the bar and onto the Gypsy. It caused the stool he sat on to let out a moan that he hoped did not mean they were about to wind up on the floor. This woman had a lot of pent-up passion that was about to be let go on the Gypsy, and he hoped that he could survive it.

He was able to corral her on top of one of the pool tables, on which she seemed surprisingly at home. The Gypsy wondered how often the pool tables saw this kind of action. The thought made him giggle a little.

"What?" the barmaid asked with a concerned look on her face.

The Gypsy chuckled a little and slowly responded, "I was just wondering how many people have done this here before," and threw an accusative look at her.

"Not recently!" she retorted hotly as she gave him a firm but playful slap to the cheek. "You better make amends for that," she stated sharply as she grabbed him firmly by both "cheeks" with her heels and pulled him in tight.

5

It approached the middle of the morning. Surely to God he had made amends for that comment. He needed to get out of there, get some food, and take his "meds."

"I've got to run, love. Are you on tonight?"

"I'm on every night, Blue-Eyes," she shot back with her smirky smile.

"Kay, later," he said. As he shot out the door, he threw up a hand.

The Gypsy first saw Chasey from across the street as he left the bar. She was picking up cans for some spare cash and trash to be a good steward. He liked that. The Gypsy watched her from the corner of his eye as he slowed his gait until she stopped to attempt to remove something stuck in a storm drain. He stopped and watched her. He looked directly at Chasey. He made no attempt to disguise the fact that he watched her. He admired the tenacity at which she went after whatever was in the drain.

While he watched her, he noticed what she wore. Chasey had on cowboy boots and very faded jeans that fit properly. Not too tight. And not too loose. Just right. You were just able to slip a finger, maybe two, in the waist band but could still tell exactly what her figure looked like. She had on a tight, plain, ribbed, gray T-shirt with a plaid print long-sleeve shirt. She had the long-sleeve shirt tied up below her braless breasts with the sleeves rolled up to her elbows. Chasey's breasts were the size and shape of slightly flattened navel oranges, perfect by the Gypsy's standards. Her dirty-blond hair was pulled back in two pigtails that stuck out from under a rolled-up, well-worn, sweaty, dusty cowgirl hat.

The only thing that kept the Gypsy from going, "Ye ha!" was the fact that she was *not* wearing "Daisy Dukes."

And then it happened. The event that changed the Gypsy's life forever. Chasey turned around and caught him as he looked at her. Okay. Let's call it what it was. The Gypsy did not look at her. He *stared* at Chasey. He was transfixed. If you loaded the Gypsy in a cannon and shot him out of town you might have diverted his stare. Pass him a napkin so he can wipe the drool from off his chin!

Chasey stood up after she failed to retrieve the shiny silver object in the storm drain to another all-too-familiar feeling of eyes upon her. She took a deep breath and turned to find—yep, another old man staring at her can. Although somehow this one seemed different. She felt her usual instant urge to give him the single-finger wave pass almost instantly, which confused her a little. She did that to every guy she slept with when she first met them. It was sort of her thing. If she even had a *thing*.

Well, the Gypsy thought, *I'm caught*.

He struggled with what to do. He quickly forced a smile. It was not the one he reserved for business but a normal smile—one that would not "freak" her out or make her think he was a "dirty ol' man"—which, of course, he was. But that was not what he wanted her "thinking." He could tell by the look on her face that she seemed a little confused. That confused the Gypsy.

Chasey watched the Gypsy struggle with his smile. She thought he was constipated the way his face looked.

Maybe he's just a lost old man looking for a restroom, she wondered as they both walked toward each other.

When they both reached the middle of the road, the Gypsy realized she was a lot shorter than she looked from across the street. Not that that was a problem. He sheepishly said, "Hi."

Chasey glanced around a few times as if she were looking for something. She looked up at the Gypsy and sputtered out, "W-wh-what are you looking at, ol' man?" She threw up both her hands in a questioning pose.

The only thing the Gypsy could think of to do was to tell the truth. So he replied, "You." And then he gave her a smile. The kind we used to give each other in grade school. Not quite a smile. Not quite a pout. But it was something that Chasey liked because she stepped up to the Gypsy, grabbed his shirt, pulled him down, and kissed him—the first of what was to become many kisses.

6

Chasey and the Gypsy stood in the middle of the three-lane road when one of the locals rolled down his window and hurled a profanity-filled tirade about them being in the middle of the road. That always pissed off the Gypsy. He lunged at the driver's car as it passed, but Chasey was able to grab him in time.

"Let him go, hun. He's not worth it," she said soothingly.

Her touch and voice had a soothing effect on the Gypsy. He apologized and said, "I'm sorry," as he shook the rage from his head. "It... just... we weren't even in his lane. The speed limit is fifteen miles per hour! AND HE DIDN'T EVEN TURN!"

Chasey reached up and touched the arm he was not using to wave frantically past them in the direction of the turn. He calmed instantly. He took a slow deep breath and stammered, "I'm... I'm... sorry. I should go." He felt dejected for losing both his temper and his chance with her.

Chasey watched him walk away. When he reached the bar, she called out, "I'll catch up with you later, Blue-Eyes."

The Gypsy threw up his hand. He did not look in her direction as he walked through the entrance to the bar. For the first time in his life, he actually *needed* a drink.

7

The Gypsy was propped up against the bar. He displayed his wares for potential customers while he listened to Jeb hurl his banter at the barmaid. His words were nothing more than insults. But he thought they were pickup lines. Jeb was a good man sober, but once he got a sip of the "devil's juice" in him, he was every woman's nightmare. And he thought he was on fire tonight. He looked to be pushing sixty. He might have been five feet six if his feet were swollen a little. And he weighed a good 250 pounds. Kinda reminded the Gypsy of Boss Hogg from the *Dukes of Hazzard* TV show just with an Elvis hairdo and minus the white tux.

Jeb owned the local car dealership. "Jeb's New & Used Cars, Trucks, Tractors & R/V's," the sign read. The Gypsy overheard people say, "You could buy anyTHING AT Jeb's." Some even went as far as to jokingly call it "Alice's Restaurant" after the Arlo Guthrie song of the same name. Maybe that's why the barmaid put up with him. She might get a car out of it.

Enterprising ol' gal, the Gypsy thought as he watched her shake her "moneymakers" at Jeb in the new top and "fancy bra" she claimed she had ordered from somewhere in New York City. She glanced over at the Gypsy and winked at him as if to ask his approval. He winked back his approval.

When the Gypsy looked back toward the doors, they blew open and in walked Nickie. Jeb whipped around on his barstool and lEt out a loud "Ha!" Nickie commenced a barrage of middle fingers and F-bombs in a slightly raspy voice hurled right at Jeb and the bunch of regulars who heckled her from the pool tables.

She was in very good shape. Extremely lean.

She must be the local aerobics instructor or fitness nut, the Gypsy thought. She reminded him of the woman who danced on the bar in the movie *Streets of Fire*. Nickie wore the shortest jean skirt he ever saw. She had the slimmest hips. Probably from being so fit. She had on six-inch stilettos the same hot pink as her lips and a lime-and-lemon tube top which covered her slightly smaller than tennis ball–sized breasts. If she were five feet tall without those shoes, it was not by much. While she had her back to the Gypsy, he noticed how nice her calves looked perched upon those heels and hoped that she might be in need of his services.

The Gypsy had always liked the calves. He especially liked men's calves for some odd reason. Why couldn't women have calves like them? They were fuller and reminded him of the shape of a heart. More so than the way the classic heart shape that was derived from a woman bending over.

Odd how some people's minds work, he thought.

After Nickie finished hurling her insults to the patrons at the pool tables, she spun around and stopped quickly and stared directly into the Gypsy's blue eyes. Her hair looked like she had hung upside-down while it dried and then gelled it to stay that way. The Gypsy could now see she had a nose ring with a chain that attached to an earring in her left ear.

Nickie continued to stare in the Gypsy's eyes as she walked up to him. She knew full well who and what he was when she ran one hand up the inside of his thigh. She grabbed hold of the business end of his money-maker, and said, "Let's get out of here, Blue-Eyes."

"If you're buyin'?" the Gypsy queried.

"Of course. Now move!" Nickie leaned in and licked him on the end of his nose.

As the Gypsy left with Nickie, the regulars serenaded them with hoots and catcalls.

Jeb was a drunken ass, but what were those other guys' problem? the Gypsy thought. *Maybe it was some kind of inside joke.*

"Hey, look. A bit of friendly advice about Jeb," Nickie started when they got in her car. "He gave Rachael a car, and ever since he thinks they're an item."

"Ya, I got that."

"So what's your deal, Blue-Eyes?"

"Just trying to make a living. You?"

"I'm just L. I. V. I. N." Nickie said. She spelled out the last word with attitude as her head slid back and forth between her shoulders.

Nickie's car was an old model import. The Gypsy couldn't tell what it used to be. She covered everything with something other than what it used to be. Somehow it worked. That was the only way to describe what she created with the car.

The Gypsy had to ask, "The car?"

"You like?"

"Why?"

"It started with just a split in the dash, and I covered it first with some decorative duct tape. Then a badge fell off outside, so I replaced it with something and then one thing led to another and here we are. Ten years later and a whole lot of stories."

The Gypsy nodded. He tried to imagine the stories behind all the applications.

They arrived at Nickie's place just outside of town as the sun began to set. She had a nice location. It was wooded, and a small stream flowed near enough. She led the Gypsy around back to the deck where she had a hammock swing hanging under the support for an old porch swing.

"You smoke, Blue-Eyes?"

"Nah, I have other vices, if you don't mind."

"No. Go ahead. I'll go roll me one and be right out. Get you a drink?"

"What kind of beer do you have?" the Gypsy asked. He hoped she had something a little more exotic than what was at the bar.

"Not much, I'm afraid. I had a party over the weekend. I've got a Guinness Extra Stout, two Ölvisholt Brugghús Lava Smoked Imperial Stout. Ooh, ooh, I've got a couple of Foothills Sexual Chocolate Imperial Stout," Nickie said seductively as she stuck her upper torso out the door. She held a stout in each hand and let them sway slightly as she licked her lips at the Gypsy.

"Sure," he said as he smiled back at her. "Let me finish up here first."

My kind of gal, he thought.

Nickie nodded and disappeared back inside. She rolled her joint and then poured the stouts into mugs she had in the freezer while the Gypsy finished taking his "meds." As the Gypsy put his sachet back, Nickie returned with their beers, her joint hanging out of her mouth, and topless. She promptly plopped herself down in the Gypsy's lap and made herself comfortable.

The Gypsy wasted no time in noticing her breasts. Nickie made sure of that. The Gypsy was not sure if they were real. He could usually tell just by looking, especially when they were on someone this lean, but hers were almost… unnatural.

Nickie leaned in and started kissing the Gypsy. He kissed her back, and as he did, he began to slide his hand under her skirt.

"Whoa!" the Gypsy said with a start as he pulled his hand back quickly.

"What's the matter, Blue-Eyes? Haven't you ever held a penis before?"

The Gypsy laughed and answered, "Yes, I've serviced many men in my career. I just didn't realize you were a transvestite." He smiled, a little embarrassed, and added, "Expecting an 'inee' but finding an 'outee,' I was just a little startled."

They both laughed at that and then got back to "business." He was really glad she laughed because he was embarrassed he had been so startled.

He thought, *I may just have to cut her a deal after that.*

8

Nickie dropped the Gypsy back at the bar a couple of hours later after they finished business. After he got out, Nickie said, "I'm having another party this weekend. Why don't you come out. Someone with your *talents* could make a lot of money," she said as she smiled wickedly up at him.

"Sure," he replied.

"It's gonna start 'round sundown Friday," Nickie said as she tossed him a wad of cash through the window after he shut the door. "I know you didn't intend to charge me after your little faux pas. Believe me, coming from a pro like you, that was the best compliment anyone could have given me," she said with a wink.

Before she pulled away, she flatly stated, "And you probably shouldn't tell Rachael about the party."

"Kay," the Gypsy replied. He gave her a little two-finger salute as she pulled away.

The Gypsy returned to the bar to a few more patrons than when he left. He found Jeb right where he left him and pretty much in the same sorry shape. If not worse.

As the Gypsy approached the bar, Jeb caught sight of him and asked, "Well, how was 'SHE'?" with a real annoying and sarcastic tone that rubbed the Gypsy the wrong way.

He stepped up to the bar in the spot next to Jeb and leaned on the bar so their eyes were the same level. Which meant the Gypsy bent down quite a bit because he was six feet three in his sock feet and tonight he wore cowboy boots with two-and-a-half-inch heels. Without blinking an eye and without yelling, but still in a fairly loud voice, he said, "'SHE' was a lady. You should be nicer to people, Jeb. One day you may need help from someone."

While the barmaid quickly made her way down to the Gypsy, he continued to stare unblinking at Jeb until Jeb began to feel uncomfortable and looked down at his drink. The Gypsy had not broken his unblinking stare on Jeb the whole time the barmaid was en route.

When she got to him, she slid him a beer and said, in a slightly worried tone, "How 'bout a beer, Blue-Eyes?"

"And a bag of nuts!" he replied with a snarl.

After he took two swigs from his beer and threw a handful of nuts into his mouth, the Gypsy finally broke his stare from Jeb, blinked, and turned to face the bar.

9

Friday night did not get here fast enough for the Gypsy. The little incident with Jeb gnawed at him. So much so, that it made him want to see Nickie to make sure she was all right. He was sure Jeb was all bark and no bite. But you never know who might have heard him and taken it upon themselves to defend Jeb's "honor."

Huh? Honor? What did any of them know about honor? the Gypsy thought derisively. He looked over at the spot where he first saw Chasey. He calmed as he thought, *Well, I'm sure there are some here that might…*

The Gypsy felt a little embarrassed that he let Jeb's bigotry and ignorance get him upset. What was it Chasey told him? "Let him go, hun. He's not worth it." And her touch. He could use her touch right now.

It was time to leave for Nickie's party. The Gypsy found a new can on the shoulder of the road and pointed it in the direction of Nickie's party. By the time he arrived at Nickie's, he forgot all about Jeb. But now he missed Chasey. He wondered if he would ever see her again and if she would even speak to him.

"Why would she?" he asked out loud. When he realized he was outside Nickie's place, he sheepishly glanced around to see if anyone was within earshot and heard his outburst. Luckily there was loud disco music blasting over speakers stuffed out the windows of her house. Everyone there was far too involved in having a good time to notice him walk up mumbling to himself anyway.

Nickie was right. It was a party. Every drag queen and transvestite within one hundred miles must have been here.

That's all right with me, the Gypsy thought with that smirky smile of his as he walked through the door. *They know how to have a good time.*

Nickie was in the kitchenette playing the good hostess. When the Gypsy walked into the place, she noticed him instantly. She ran up to him, and after she climbed him like a tree, she kissed him like he wore a black leather jacket and she was Pinky Tuscadero. Or maybe it was just the pink cowgirl boots, pink *very* short shorts, and white button-up shirt she had tied between her breasts that had him a little confused. Nickie even had a pink handkerchief that held her hair back that completed the ensemble. It all made him want to give her a thumbs-up when she finally climbed down.

"Blue-Eyes! You made it!" Nickie squealed with glee as she bounced up and down and back and forth. Her actions almost reminded the Gypsy of a Jack Russel terrier.

Maybe she was wanting a little treat? the Gypsy thought as he watched her bound around.

"You look a might cute tonight, Miss Nickie," he said as she grabbed his hand.

"Come on. I'll introduce you."

As she dragged him by his arm quickly away from the entrance, he thought, *We must look like a child dragging their father around to show him the latest 'I GOTTA HAVE THIS NOW!' item to have just hit the toy store shelves.*

First, they briefly stopped by a nice group of queens. Nickie used air quotes and said that they were from "out of town," whatever that was supposed to mean. *Why do people do that?* The Gypsy wondered. *Just say "They're from out of town." 'cause if I don't know them, it don't matter. And what's with everybody using those damn air quotes?*

Then they stopped at a group in the kitchenette who talked about their new tattoos and showed the tattoos to them. Someone outside called for Nickie. She popped out the door in a flash and left the Gypsy to his own vices. As fate would have it, there was a little group in the corner with the kind of *vice* he wanted.

The Gypsy rubbed his hands together and "smacked" his lips. *I guess that's why they call it* smack, he thought with a smile as he started to move toward the group until someone caught his attention in the corner of his eye and completely derailed his plans.

There stood Chasey. Right there on Nickie's deck. She was looked at him and smiled an odd smile.

Wait. Why was she smiling? the Gypsy wondered. *Is my fly down?* A quick, discreet check revealed that it was up, but those checks are never discreet. *So what's she smiling at?* he kept wondering. He finally decided to walk over and ask her since she did not seem intent to come in and join him. On his way out, it occurred to him. *She's just doing to me what I did to her when we first met. So I will know how it feels to have someone stare at me with a goofy grin on their face,* he thought. A little "taste of his own medicine."

"I'm likin' you more every time I see you, young'un," he said as he finally got close enough to Chasey to be heard over the music.

Chasey smiled her best toothy grin back up at the Gypsy as she led him over to the railing. She promptly hopped up on the railing. She swung the Gypsy around in front of her so they faced each other. She hooked her heels behind his thighs and pulled him in tight. Unfortunately, the Gypsy's knees went in between the railing stiles, and he almost fell backward. Chasey grabbed his wrists and leaned back. Her actions allowed him to regain his balance and grab onto the rail. They both took a deep breath as they regained their respective composures. Then Chasey reached up with both hands and started kissing the Gypsy. Nothing too serious. Just your normal make-out kissing.

The Gypsy moved his hands from the rail and started past her bottom. They just hovered above her bottom but did not touch her. He paused there for only a second before he moved his hands up to her back. He placed them there where they respectfully remained.

Chasey stopped kissing the Gypsy for a moment and pulled back to look into his eyes. She thought, *Could it just be a job for him? Could we have a relationship based on love and not sex?*

The Gypsy looked back at her very confused, so she thought she should say something. Instead she kissed him more passionately than she ever kissed anyone in her life. And the Gypsy reciprocated.

ARTOOLLIOUS

Nickie informed all the guests that the food was ready to be served as she approached where Chasey and the Gypsy were involved in their romantic enterprise. As she passed the Gypsy and Chasey, she gave them a little nudge and said, "Get a room."

10

Most of the guests had migrated out to the back where Nickie had hired a couple of her friends to cater the party. The caterers were a stereotypical gay "bear" couple dressed in matching flannel T-shirts and bib overall shorts. They both had full black beards and full heads of not quite shoulder-length, wavy hair. They wore gray and red wool socks that peaked above some very expensive-looking hiking boots on their very hairy legs. They were both stocky as bears should be, but neither would be considered fat.

What's with all the stereotypes? the Gypsy wondered. *We've got the bears in flannel. The queens all lookin' like Liza, Babs, or Cher.* He felt a rant coming on. He thought, *I'll bet she wouldn't invite a bunch of black people and then serve them waterm*—as he turned to where Chasey walked beside him, he gestured broadly with his arm as he was about to begin his rant. That was when he noticed the group of black people. They sat around a small fire and ate watermelon.

The sight caused the Gypsy to stop in full pose. His frozen stance made him look like he was a hunting dog that pointed toward its prey. He was completely surprised to see a group of stoned and/or drunk black people actually eating watermelon. His look was even more outlandish with his mouth slightly agape as he was about to begin a rant on the idiocy of purposefully supporting stereotypes. The only quick save the Gypsy could come up with was to nod, smile, and switch the point to more of a weak wave. It seemed to work. Because while watermelon juice ran down their chins and dripped off their hands, the group responded in kind with big, toothy smiles and stoned waves of their own.

This caused the Gypsy to scoff even more. His actions made Chasey ask, "What's wrong? What are you looking for?" as the Gypsy looked wildly around.

"What am I looking for?" he asked in a near panic, it seemed. "What am I looking FOR?" he almost screamed. "I'll tell you what I'm looking for. I'm looking for Mel Brooks," he finally said as he let his flailing arms fall flatly against his sides.

Chasey looked at him like he had completely lost his mind. She then asked, "Who?"

"Mel Brooks. Or maybe Rachael Feinstein. You know. The obligatory stereotypical Jewish comedian. We've got just about everything else covered here." He started flapping his arms as he ranted. That action, along with his raised voice, drew everyone's attention.

Chasey walked closer to him and placed a calming hand on his rapidly heaving chest. She lightly patted him on his chest and asked, "What the hell are you talking about, Blue-Eyes?"

"Well…" the Gypsy started, unaware his antics drew attention. "Look around. We have practically EVERY stereotype here but the Jewish comic—the Bible beater in the polyester suit telling everybody not to judge but we're all going to go to hell, and the bleach-blonde airheads with springs for necks, and I think just about every stereotype would be represented."

"We definitely have the 'crazy old man' department well represented. How much of your,"—Chasey cleared her throat and continued—"'meds' have you had?" she asked. She knew full well he had not had so much as a drop to drink since he arrived.

The Gypsy's arms dropped to his side in a huff as everyone burst into a raucous round of laughter. He just snarled at Chasey as Nickie walked by them. As she passed them, she patted the Gypsy on the back and complained, "Seriously, guys. Get a room." The Gypsy cut Nickie a disapproving glance.

Chasey patted the Gypsy's chest one more time and then said, "Come on, let's grab a bite, and then we'll get out of here." And with that, he did as he was told.

11

Chasey and the Gypsy sat on the ground in front of a log by a fire. While they enjoyed each other's company, they picked at what was left of the BBQ they just finished. It was a variety of wild game on top of your normal brisket and chicken the bear twins smoked up for the group. This was real BBQ. Not just meat thrown upon a grill and covered with sauce; the Bear Twins started smoking everything the previous night. They even smoked the baked beans somehow. The Gypsy had to admit that they were the best damn beans he ever tried. He also liked the rattlesnake.

Chasey watched the Gypsy's interactions with everyone since he arrived and noticed a great many things about his personality.

I guess those psychology classes are still sticking with me, she thought.

She took particular interest in the way he looked at people when he spoke to them. He either would not look directly at someone when he spoke to them or he would stare directly into their eyes for uncomfortably long periods. She wondered if he had ever been diagnosed with Asperger's syndrome and decided to ask.

"Have you ever heard of Asperger's syndrome?

"Gazuntite!" the Gypsy replied.

"Cute. I'm serious."

"Yes. Why, do you think I have it too?"

"When I got my degree in PT, I minored in psychology. So I notice things sometimes. You exhibit some symptoms."

"Well, I am asexual. So there's a good probability."

"Really!" Chasey responded in delight. She took a deep breath and added, "So am I."

"Why are you so excited by that?" the Gypsy asked, confused by her giddy reply.

"Because it means…" And then she leaned in and kissed him again like she had never kissed anyone before.

Nickie walked by Chasey and the Gypsy as they sat and stared dreamily into each other's eyes. She said in a huffy tone as she passed, "I thought I told you two to get a room?" She threw up her arms and shook her head in disbelief as she stormed off.

"Come on," Chasey said as she stood and wiped the ground from her jeans. "I did say we'd leave after we ate, didn't I?"

She did, in fact. The Gypsy had not taken his "meds" today. He found that he did not care if he did. He would rather be with Chasey. He also realized he did not hurt as bad when they were together. She helped him up, and while they stood there, they looked deeply into each other's eyes. Chasey reached up and pulled the Gypsy down to her, and they began their kissing… again. Something that would become a recurring theme in their lives every time she would look deeply into his eyes.

Those eyes, Chasey thought as she kissed him deeply and passionately. *My eyes!* She squeezed him tightly, and he picked her up; as he did, she wrapped her legs around his hips.

12

The only reason Chasey and the Gypsy knew the fire went out was that they started to get cold as they stood there alone next to where the fire once burned as it kept the cold desert night at bay. That was when they realized they were alone. They were too involved in each other to notice everyone went indoors, so no one was there to feed the fire.

Chasey and the Gypsy tried to decide what to do. As they stood there and shivered like two teenagers in love, Nickie came outside and checked for party-goers who did not make it inside safely. As she made her sweep of the property, she shook her head at them. She watched them as they shivered from the cold while they stared into each other's eyes. As she passed behind where they stood, she grabbed them both by their belt-loops. She ushered them toward the road and said, "I thought I told you two to GET A ROOM!" She gave them both a loving farewell push and said, "Do I need to buy you condoms as well?"

They both gave her a single-finger salute for that comment.

As the Gypsy and Chasey walked down the road, they arrived a a truck, and she said, "This one's mine."

She opened the driver's side door to her 1939 Dodge step-s' pickup and slid into the passenger side along the long, thick b' leather seat. The Gypsy stepped up onto the running board climbed inside. The roomy interior of the older models always his larger frame. When he rode in Nickie's car, he felt like he a clown car. Even with the seat pushed all the way back, his k the dash. After one particularity painful bump, he actually about asking her if he could take the seat out and ride in t'

"You have to double-clutch it," Chasey said as the Gypsy started it up using the floor starter.

After the Gypsy started the truck and put it in gear, Chasey slid over next to him as they pulled out onto the road. As they headed down the road, the old Mopar flathead 6 chugged away at forty miles per hour. They had the vent windows cocked to let in the desert night air and to let the exhaust fumes out also. It was not fancy, but it was well cared for and loved.

The Gypsy looked down at her and smiled. Chasey realized he was staring at her and said, "Watch the road, Blue-Eyes."

"Sorry, I don't normally drive," he apologized as his head snapped back around to watch the road.

"You do have a license, don't you?" she asked with genuine concern.

"Yes, yes," he said hurriedly as he patted her thigh. "And it's valid too."

"Okay," she chuckled. "It's the next left. About three more miles."

He made the left without incident and brought the truck to a stop in the drive of a nice little adobe house. It was a spacious two-[roo]m home with an outbuilding in back. Chasey had a large area of [b]ack fenced in to contain various farm animals she maintained for [her] needs. She would sell extra goods to make a few extra dollars.

[Afte]r they got inside, Chasey asked, "It's late. Do you want a

[The Gyp]sy raised his arm, sniffed, and said, "I'm fine," and [smiled at] the eighth-grader who had just made the joke.

[Chasey] shook her head and said, "Come on, Blue-Eyes."

[They lay] together on the Murphy bed she pulled from the [wall. Chasey asked] the Gypsy if he needed to shower. The Gypsy [said no. This] would be the first good night's sleep he would [ever ho]ld remember. As Chasey lay there, she tried to [recall if] she just slept with a man before *she* slept with [him befo]re and contemplated those thoughts while [sleep. A]s they drifted off to sleep.

13

Chasey and the Gypsy were awakened just before dawn to pecking and scratching at the back door. Chasey pushed the Gypsy out of the bed. She moaned, "Ohh, go see what they want." And then she rolled back into the bed.

The Gypsy staggered toward the door. He scratched his head and wondered, *"Who could it be at this hour?"* Then it hit him. Where he was.

See what they want? Is she on drugs? the Gypsy thought with a chuckle and a shake of his head.

He opened the door to find some guinea fowl pecking and clawing at the door. The Gypsy turned to Chasey and said, "I think they want you to fix *them* FOR breakfast."

Chasey mumbled "What?" and then a guinea fowl let out one of its high-pitched shrill calls that brought her right out of bed. She Screamed, "Why the hell did you let them in the house, Blue-Eyes?"

She stomped her feet and flailed her arms wildly as she drove the guinea fowl out the door the Gypsy held open. The Gypsy started horselaughing at the sight of Chasey flailing her arms and legs in the nude as she was. She grabbed the door from him and gently closed it. She pulled him down, gave him an evil chuckle and a peck on the lips as they headed back to bed.

14

Chasey and the Gypsy watered and fed the large variety of small farm "critters" she had around the property. After they finished the morning chores, they sat down to a nice breakfast of fresh greens, citrus, some duck and chicken eggs and some of "Chasey's secret recipe lamb-and-goat sausage."

Yep, it tastes a little like a lamb and a goat, the Gypsy thought. It was edible (sort of), just *not* pork sausage. *Nothing beats good old pork sausage*, he thought. The more he thought about it, the more he really did want some good old pork sausage. And the more he thought about it, the *less* he liked the lamb/goat sausage.

"How do you like the sausage?" Chasey asked.

The Gypsy thought about how to respond. He thought about how a kind lie might be considerate. But he did not want to start this relationship lying to her. Not even over something as trivial as this terrible sausage.

He replied, "It's not my cup of tea, really. A little too gamy."

"Thanks for being honest, Blue-Eyes. Most guys would say they love it just to be nice or because they want to get into my pants." She reached out and touched his hand and smiled lovingly at him. At that moment she knew she wanted to spend the rest of her life with him.

The Gypsy looked back at her and smiled in return. He wondered, *What was that all about?* as he finished his breakfast.

As they finished washing the dishes and put everything away, the Gypsy asked, "If you're gonna be in town around lunch, stop by the bar and we'll go grab a bite somewhere."

"Okay. I have some scrap and recycling to pick up and deliver this morning. I'll be back around 1:00 p.m. I could use your help with the breakdown of the new stuff I bring back," Chasey asked, as she batted her eyes flirtatiously at him. She hoped to convince him to come home with her and keep him away from that whore Rachael.

"Sure, no problem," he said, as he tossed the hand towel he used to dry the clean dishes playfully into her face.

The Gypsy gathered up the couple of things he had, including his sachet with his "meds." As he tucked the sachet away in his pocket, he realized he had not taken them since earlier the day before.

What has she done to me? he thought.

He was not sure if he approved yet, but the thought of the "possibility" of approval made him smile.

He was still smiling as he looked back at Chasey. As he headed out the door, he said, "Be safe out there. Hope I get to see you later."

"Kay. If not, I'll catch up with you this evenin'," Chasey replied and waved bye as she did.

The Gypsy threw up his hand as he walked out the door, and just before the door shut, Chasey called out sarcastically, "Give Rachael my *best*."

15

The Gypsy arrived back at the bar before it opened. Rachael leaned on the bar and read her newspaper as she sipped on her morning coffee with one hand and held a half-finished cigarette in the other. She glanced up with her eyes to see who *dared* disturb her morning. She shot upright when she saw who it was.

With an accusative stare and snarky tone, she called out to him from across the bar, "And just where have YOU been?"

"None of your business, MOM!" he shot back over his shoulder as he stowed his things. The Gypsy spun around slowly on the ball of his right foot and stood up. He gave the barmaid a little look of his own as if to say, "Two can play this game."

As he walked around the bar to where she stood, he nodded to where Jeb was usually positioned and asked, "Where's *you*r boyfriend?"

The Gypsy walked seductively with a slightly disgusted snarl on his face to complement the one of hate and discontent that now adorned the barmaid's face as he approached her. When he was within striking distance, the barmaid grabbed the Gypsy and pulled them both down onto the floor behind the bar.

The barmaid was thoroughly enjoying herself as she made the Gypsy pay his rent. Just as she got to the point of "collecting the rent" she liked best, someone walked into the bar.

"Cain't you read? We're closed, DAMN IT!" the barmaid screamed.

The footsteps did not hesitate at her command. They continued and came right up to the bar. They stopped at the edge, and Sheriff Winnemucca peered over the bar. He was a fairly short man and supposedly a direct descendant of the war chief of the Kuyuidika band of the Paiute Tribe of Native American Indians, Winnemucca the Younger. Winnemucca the Younger was rumored to not like the white settlers, but according to everyone in town, the sheriff was one of the best all-around people you would ever want to meet. He would go out of his way to help anyone. Supposedly…

"Sorry to interrupt your morning… *constitutional*, Rachael, but I need to talk to you a minute," the sheriff apologetically said.

The Gypsy sat back against the cooler with his jeans still around his ankles. He just sat there and looked at the sheriff with his arms on his knees while the barmaid covered herself and asked the sheriff, "What's so damn important?"

After the sheriff finished looking the Gypsy over, who still just sat there and made no effort to pull up his pants or even try to cover himself, he looked at the barmaid and said, "It's about your brother—I mean, your *sister*."

"Oh God! What's that IDIOT done now?" she screamed as she threw her hands up in the air.

"He…"—the sheriff shook his head—"SHE was seen with some of her friends out near the reservation again."

"Oh, good grief! Doesn't she know they'll kill her if they catch her stealing artifacts again?" the barmaid screeched. She grabbed the bar and jumped up to meet the sheriff.

"I can only do so much to keep the council placated. If they catch her snooping around, whether she has anything or not…" the sheriff paused to think of how best to word the importance of what he said next. "Rachael, you need to make Nickie understand. I'm the one she wants to get caught by, NOT someone on the reservation," the sheriff finished what he had to say and rapped his knuckles on the bar to emphasize the point.

The sheriff turned, walked out of the bar and left the barmaid and the Gypsy to their vices. As the barmaid mulled over what to do about Nickie, the Gypsy thought, *That explains where Nickie got her money and a lot of the things she had. She was a "tomb raider,"* the Gypsy thought. He almost laughed but held it in, under the circumstances.

The barmaid took a couple of deep breaths, turned around, and looked at the Gypsy with a crooked smile and said, "Well, now you know one more of my secrets. Let's get you back to work." She jumped back on the Gypsy. They kissed as he removed her clothing, and he went back to work "paying the rent."

Later that day, after the Gypsy finished "paying the rent," he propped himself up at the bar. While he read the paper, the barmaid tended to the handful of afternoon customers that were in the bar. A large, wide, dumb-looking local walked up to the Gypsy and struck up a conversation that seemed a bit odd to him. He saw this character in the bar several times before with some people that he was sure he heard were "family" of some sort. *Cousins,* he thought. And if he remembered correctly, everybody said to watch them. They were all thieves. And very good ones.

"Don't I know you? Weren't we in Joliet together?"

"Don't think so," the Gypsy flatly replied without looking up from his paper.

"I know you from somewhere," the diversion prodded further.

"Probably just here."

"Oh," he said as he stepped over and blocked the Gypsy from being able to have a straight-line view of where his things were stored. "That's it, I guess," he added. He continued on with general-weather type of chitchat which the Gypsy ignored.

Then he asked something that caught the Gypsy's undivided attention, "Aren't you worried about someone stealing your things?"

"Nah," the Gypsy responded like he was uninterested. "I always keep them in sight. And if I can't see 'em, I have someone I can trust watching 'em."

At that moment the barmaid pulled her shotgun from under the bar and ratcheted a shell into the chamber and yelled out, "EVAN CHAMBERS, YOU GET AWAY FROM THAT, YOU THIEVING SON OF A BITCH!"

"Friend of yours?" the Gypsy asked of the diversion. He stared directly in the diversion's eyes with a look that was just a little unsettling.

"Not anymore," he replied and swallowed hard.

"Ya... right," the Gypsy kicked with lightning speed directly at the knee the diversion had all his weight on. The kick caused it to make a loud crack. After the diversion hit the floor, he let out a scream that sounded a lot like a little five-year-old with a skinned knee.

As the Gypsy slowly rose from his seated position and prepared to do God knows what, the barmaid called out, "THAT'S ENOUGH, BLUE-EYES! MIKE, BILLY, DRAG FAT BOY OUTSIDE! THE SHERIFF'S ON HIS WAY."

She knew this was so because she tripped her silent alarm. Since this was an old mining town, the jail was right across the street from the saloon. The sheriff or one of his deputies just needed to cross the street to get there. "AND YOU JUST START MOVING TOWARD THE DOOR NICE AND SLOW, EVAN."

The sheriff stepped through the doors of the bar as Rachael led Evan in the direction of the exit with her shotgun. When he saw the shotgun pointed in his direction, he ducked and asked, "Ms. Rachael, you mind puttin' that scattergun down and lettin' me take it from here?"

"Sorry, Sheriff," she replied as she lowered the gun. "You and your kin all stay out of here from now on, Evan. "YOU HEAR ME?" she yelled as she pointed her finger at Evan. While the sheriff took Evan by the collar, Mike and Billy dragged the cousin out the door as he squalled and clutched his knee.

"Thanks," the Gypsy shot over to the barmaid. She just nodded.

16

It was around lunch one afternoon. The barmaid busied herself with the count of the cash drawer after the Gypsy had "paid his rent". He was propped up at the bar as he skimmed through the newspaper when Chasey opened the door to the bar. She placed one foot inside the bar. A spiteful smile adorned her face as she looked past the Gypsy at the barmaid.

The Gypsy spun around and saw Chasey as she stood just inside the door. He got up, threw up a hand and hollered, "Later."

The barmaid and Chasey exchanged hateful glances as the Gypsy approached the door. As he passed Chasey, he used an outstretched arm and politely swept her out the door with him.

As they turned down the sidewalk toward the parking lot, the Gypsy thought, *I'll have to find out about this feud when the time is right. I don't need to be in the middle of just another catfight, let alone something more sinister.*

As they turned the corner, Chasey grabbed the Gypsy by his arm. She spun him sideways and jerked him to a stop so quickly that he almost fell. He maintained his balance on one leg and kept himself from falling down. She looked up into his eyes and then looked down like a dog that had just been scolded.

She took a deep breath and then said, "I guess you noticed Rachael and I have a bit of a history."

"I noticed a bit of tension there," he replied in a slightly mocking tone as he moved his shoulders and hands from side to side in a mocking fashion.

Chasey looked at him, blinked and smiled sheepishly as if to imply "Okay, Capt'n Obvious."

She continued with her explanation as she gently patted the Gypsy's chest.

"When I was in high school, I was dating a boy I thought I was going to marry. We weren't going to have sex until we got married. Then Rachael comes to town and uses her body to manipulate everyone to get *everything* she wants. She was an older woman who offered him sex, and he took it. After she was done with him, she threw him aside. He thought he was 'in love' just because she had sex with him." She paused and took a deep breath before she continued. "He shot himself."

She had to stop for a second. While she paused, she leaned in and hugged the Gypsy. He held her lightly and gently stroked her hair back, which he followed with a kiss to the top of her head.

Chasey continued her story as they started toward the truck. "I don't know why, but she has been after every man I ever dated until I lost my virginity. Then she left them alone. I know it sounds crazy," she said as she shook her head and backed away. "But I SWEAR, after I lost it, she NEVER hit on another one of my boyfriends again."

The Gypsy looked at her kind of sideways and asked, "Have you been in love with any of the people you had sex with?"

Chasey was silent, but she looked like she had been slapped. When the truth finally settled in, she ran back into the Gypsy and hugged him tightly. It was such a tight hug that it caused him to wince a little in pain. Chasey realized that she squeezed him to tightly and caused him pain. She let go and said, "I'm sorry. We have to get out of here. Come away with me."

Was it the pain in his back, or was it what she asked him to do that made him feel light-headed and sick to his stomach?

"I... I... need to think about it," he stammered. "Let's get a bite to eat and talk."

He hadn't said no. That's good enough for now, Chasey thought. She nodded in confirmation as they walked to the truck. She got in on the driver's side and slid across for the Gypsy to get in and drive.

As they pulled out of the parking lot, the Gypsy asked Chasey, "What do you feel like having for lunch?"

She looked up at him and asked, "Is it all right with you if we go back to my place so we can have some privacy?"

He nodded okay and then added as he put his arm around her and pulled her in tight, "Sure."

As they pulled into Chasey's driveway, the Gypsy noticed the large pile of recyclable material Chasey "dragged" back to be broken down. Somewhere she found an old steam shovel of some kind.

He looked at her dumbfounded after he brought the truck to a stop and asked, "Did you bring that home with this?"

"Well, I sure didn't strap it to Gracie [Gracie being her milking goat] and drag it here!" she snapped back and smiled.

"This thing's got more *umph* than I would've guessed. Where did you find that?" he asked, as he jerked a thumb at the steam shovel.

"You can find those old things everywhere around old mine and construction sites if you know where to look. And if you know whom to ask and how, you can get it for free, to boot," she said with a wink and a smile.

Oh my god, the Gypsy thought. *She's just a glorified tomb raider. Is this another sticking point between her and the barmaid?* He had to resist the overwhelming urge to laugh. And he really wanted to laugh right now. So bad, in fact, he bit the inside of his mouth.

Then Chasey's tone changed, and she said, "When I first met Nickie, she hadn't started taking hormones yet. She went by Nick then. The two of us would scrounge for recyclables together and split the profits." She paused as they went inside to fix their lunch.

"He'd met some transvestites, and then *he* started hormones. After that, *he* changed. Somewhere *she* met someone who told her about an old Paiute Indian burial mound that you could get a lot of valuable treasure from if you got into one. Nickie tried to talk me into joining them, but I told them, warned them, about how the tribes protect their burial sites. Plus it's against the LAW!" she added. She shook her head and stabbed angrily at her mesclun and spinach salad.

Chasey continued, "We both made really good money legally. Why go and do that? But all of them got caught. The sheriff was able to negotiate a deal to keep Nickie out of serious trouble. Rachael always blamed me."

Chasey paused for a moment. While she thought how to continue, the Gypsy reached over and placed his hand on her hand to comfort her.

She looked up and continued, "She blames me for turning him into a criminal and for turning him trans. She thinks I did it all in revenge for what she did to me." Then Chasey burst into tears.

The Gypsy got up, moved over to her, swept her up into his arms and held her. He thought as he held her, *I need to get her away from here. Soon.*

17

After Chasey and the Gypsy finished cleaning the lunch dishes and put the kitchen back in order, Chasey said, "If you became my business partner, you would be able to stop turning tricks."

The Gypsy never called what he did "turning tricks". For some reason, that term always had a dirty, filthy connotation to him that he disliked, and when Chasey said it the way she did, it was like a slap in the face. He wasn't "dirty." He was kind and caring. He wasn't "filthy." He was loving and gentle.

The Gypsy took a deep breath and said uncomfortably, "Let's take a look at that shovel."

"Not right now. I need to go check on another job before dark. Do you want to come with me?" Chasey asked hopefully.

He almost said yes, but instead answered, "I would, but I'm expecting someone later. Around five this evening. How long would we be?"

"We won't make it back by then. Will I see you tonight?" she asked. She hoped he would decide to come and stay with her for good.

"Kay," he replied with a kind and loving smile.

"Come on, Blue-Eyes. Let's get you back to the bar so I can get down the road."

They started what was now routine to them: Chasey climbed into the driver's side, slid across to the passenger side, the Gypsy got in, started the truck, etc.

They rode down the highway toward the bar as they enjoyed each other's company. Chasey hung on the Gypsy's arm. She looked up into "those eyes," as he glanced for cross traffic at the upcoming intersection. She really hoped he would decide to stay with her and that he would decide to do it tonight.

As they pulled up next to the bar and stopped, Chasey asked as the Gypsy got out, "Do you want me to come by and get you later?"

"I'm not sure where I'll be when. But you can stop by when you get back. What time?"

"Prolly 'bout ten unless there's unforeseen traffic problems."

"Kay. I'll try to be here unless I'm with a customer," the Gypsy said. As he headed toward the bar door, he threw up a hand and waved goodbye.

18

The Gypsy came through the bar doors just after 3:00 p.m. to an empty barroom save the barmaid. As he headed toward where he had his things stashed, he threw up his hand at the barmaid as she looked up to see who it was.

Upon seeing that it was the Gypsy, the barmaid shouted out, "Did you fuck her?"

He did not need to see the sneering scowl of hatred and contempt that adorned her face to know the poison that dripped off her tongue at this moment. He could hear it in her voice. And that was all he needed to know. Chasey told the truth.

The Gypsy spun around quickly and stormed up to the bar. He threw his bag over his shoulder as he went. When he made it to the bar, he slammed both palms down on it. His action caused the barmaid to pull the shotgun from under the bar, cock it, and point it directly in the Gypsy's face in one smooth, quick action. An action that looked like she practiced it many times.

He said as he stared straight down the barrel of the barmaid's semiautomatic Beretta 12-gauge shotgun, "We did not have sex. And even *if* we did, IT IS NONE OF YOUR DAMN BUSINESS!" He made last part as loud as he was able. When the barmaid told others about the event, she swore that the whole place shook.

"GET OUT! AND STAY OUT, YOU CRAZY SON OF A BITCH! DON'T YOU OR THAT CONNIVING SLUT EVER SET FOOT IN HERE AGAIN!" the barmaid screeched.

The Gypsy thought about giving her the single-finger salute as he exited but let the door gently close behind him instead. As the Gypsy walked down the sidewalk, he felt pretty proud with the way he handled everything, Jeb stepped around the corner of the building as he headed toward the bar to start his evening of drinking.

Jeb saw the Gypsy was smiling and in a good mood. He threw up his hand to say hello the way the Gypsy always did and said, "Afternoon."

The Gypsy threw up his hand in kind reply. He said, "She could use a friend right about now." As they passed, he gave Jeb a pat on his shoulder.

Well, the Gypsy thought, *I wonder if he'll step up and be a good friend or take advantage of the situation like the worm that he is.* The Gypsy kinda hoped he would be the worm.

The Gypsy sat down on the bench at the corner and waited for his 5:00 p.m. appointment to arrive. While he sat there, he thought about going back to Chasey's to wait for her afterward, but if she came here first… well, that could get ugly. He decided after he finished with this customer, he would just come back here and wait for her.

Just before 5:00 p.m., Nickie showed up driving a rat rod the likes of which the Gypsy had never seen. It looked to be a '70s model Jeep CJ5 that had oversized tires with a widened and stretched footprint. It looked to have no more than six inches of ground clearance but still sported thirty-eight-inch "mudders" all around. It had a big block Chevy with headers and pipes sticking straight up through the hood. It was a "little" loud. And the cherry on top, Nickie had it painted her favorite color of pink. If you could not hear her coming, you should be able to see her.

The Gypsy sat on the bench with his fingers in his ears. Nickie stopped in front of him, gave a whistle and then shouted, "Hop in, Blue-Eyes."

The Gypsy chuckled as he shook his head. "Right on time. Where'd you find this?" he yelled as he climbed into the Jeep.

"This was something I put together with Chasey's help a few years ago. I've got a couple of good friends waiting for us when we get home. I hope you're up for it?" Nickie asked with a coy grin.

"As long as you're buyin', I am."

After the Gypsy got settled into the pink, leopard skin–lined bucket seats and strapped in with the five-point harness, which he hoped was the last time he would be wearing a harness tonight, they tore off down the road with the unmistakable roar of Detroit Muscle and the smell of burning rubber. In a word, this thing was *dangerous*.

As the two of them roared down the highway in the Jeep, the Gypsy thought he should tell Nickie about what happened between him and the barmaid. While he was at it, he could get Nickie's side of all the events he heard about.

"Can you pull over a minute. I need to talk to you about something before we get to your place," the Gypsy yelled over the loud exhaust. Nickie nodded and pulled over. She shut the beast down after she brought it to a stop.

The Gypsy started quickly and bluntly. "Your sister's mad at me."

"Well, let's see, my sister being mad at you could only be about one of two things. Either Chasey or… MOI?" Nickie asked after a slight hesitation.

"Well, to be honest… she's pissed. She told me to never come back."

"BOTH of us!" Nickie squealed with pleasure. "Oh, tell me everything," she pleaded like a little schoolgirl who awaited the latest gossip from her BFF.

The Gypsy relayed to Nickie what happened between him and Rachael and why. He also told her about the sheriff stopping by and asked if what the sheriff said was true.

After a deep inhale and exhale, Nickie said, "Partially, I did go and try to rob a grave site the first time, but I learned my lesson. I DID NOT go back after that. EVER! I haven't even seen the other two I went with the first time since. Nor do I want to. Okay?"

"Fair enough," the Gypsy said. "I just wanted to get this settled before we got back since you have others there. Plus, this will be our last time together."

Nickie just stared at the Gypsy in stunned silence. Then she slowly smiled when she realized what he meant. "Oh, Blue-Eyes!" Nickie gushed. "I'm so happy for you two." She reached over to hug him, but she forgot she was strapped into the bucket seat by the five-point restraints and almost choked herself. As her head popped back, she started laughing.

The Gypsy said, "I need to be sure to be back at the bar by 9:00 p.m. Chasey said she would be back by 10:00 p.m., and I don't want her to get back to the bar early and run into your sister."

"Ya, that probably wouldn't be good. No worries. Gizellae and Cierra are leaving at 7:00 p.m. anyway. That will give us some time alone… to talk," she said with a gentle smile as she touched his hand just before she fired up the pink demon and tore back down the highway.

19

Nickie returned the Gypsy to the bar just before 9:00 p.m. as promised. As he got out of Nickie's old work-of-art car, she gave him one final loving pat on the backside goodbye. As she playfully shook her shoulders back and forth to accentuate her chest for him that was lovingly displayed in a leopard-print push-up bra that peeked out above a black V-neck T-shirt, she said, "I'm going to miss our playtime together. You're the best-aged vino I've ever had."

The Gypsy leaned back in, kissed Nickie, and said, "Me too."

As the Gypsy leaned back out of the car, Nickie grabbed his hand and slapped a large wad of cash into his palm. "A gift for Chasey and you to get the two of you started on your life together. I know I don't have to say this, but be good to her. Please?"

"You know I will." He leaned back in and kissed Nickie one final time goodbye and then shut the door. "Thank you, Nickie. For everything. I'm sure we'll see you again before we move on."

"Ciao, Blue-Eyes," Nickie said with a final wave goodbye as she pulled away.

The Gypsy threw up his hand as Nickie drove away. He walked over to the bench, sat down and waited for Chasey.

20

Chasey arrived back at the bar just as the Gypsy started to get uncomfortable. She slowed and asked, "Want me to park an' go in an' get a beer?"

The Gypsy shook his head no as he got up with his things and said, "Nope. We should go home." He threw his things in the bed of the truck as he walked around the back.

It did not strike Chasey immediately what the Gypsy said or even *meant*. But it did when he stepped up to get in the truck, and she started to shake, so much so the Gypsy noticed.

"What's wrong?" he asked.

"Just a little chill." She fibbed and then hugged him tight. "I… I… it was just what you said, the way you said it." She paused briefly and then looked up sheepishly and continued, "I just wasn't expecting you to ever settle down. I hope we don't make too many mistakes."

The Gypsy held up "two" fingers and tried to act like a Scout. With a goofy look on his face, he said in a childish voice, "I promise to stop one mistake short of too many."

"Okay, 'Dennis the Menace to Society,' you're supposed to have 'three' fingers to be a good Scout," she said and gave him a little tweak on his nose. "Let's go home."

The Gypsy closed the door. He backed the truck out of the parking lot and headed down the road the short trip to *their* home. On the way he explained what transpired between him and the barmaid, being sure to leave out the part with the shotgun. Chasey blew her top, understandably so, but the Gypsy managed to calm her down and asked, "I want you to promise me you will stay away from her."

She looked right up into his big deep blue eyes and said, "Yes, Blue-Eyes. I promise." Chasey leaned up and kissed him just in time for them to make the turn into the drive. "But if she comes lookin' for trouble… I'm makin' no DAMN promises!" Chasey said loudly as she stuck her finger in his face to emphasize her point.

"I'm fine with that," he said after he kissed the end of her finger since she seemed intent on leaving it in his face. "Just, if you see her out…" he paused as he tried to choose his words correctly. He continued, "Try to be on the opposite side of the road." He stared down into her eyes with a little crooked smirk. "Try to be the more mature person. I may have lost MY temper and said things I probably shouldn't have. That doesn't mean we have to go and be mean. Leave her be."

"Okay, Blue-Eyes. I promise."

After Chasey's promise, the Gypsy kissed her on the forehead, and they climbed out of the old Dodge. "How'd it go this evenin'?" he asked after he shut the door behind Chasey.

"Great! We've got to break this thing up tout de suite," she exclaimed as she motioned to the old steam shovel she brought home earlier. "I have people coming to get most of this stuff next week. But we have to make room for the new drill machines. I've got fifty-two of them! And the property owner wants them off in a week."

"Can we get that many in a week?"

"Sure. It's just having enough space to store them that's going to be the trick. Nickie will probably help. I'll call her in the morning."

The mention of Nickie's name reminded him of her gift to them. "That reminds me," he started as he pulled a large wad of money from his duffel bag. "This is from Nickie. She said it was a gift. To help us get started on our new life together," he presented the large wad of bills to Chasey like a bouquet of flowers.

Chasey took the money form the Gypsy. She looked shocked as she asked, "Did Nickie give YOU all of this?"

"No. Not all of it. Most of it is mine. What I've earned… working." He looked back at her quizzically and asked, "What?" He placed both hands on his hips and continued, "Did you think I was some 'blow a drunk for a buck' whore? I get $500 an hour, MINIMUM!"

With the *minimum*, Chasey's jaw dropped to her chest with an almost-audible *thud*. Her arms dropped with such force that she almost dropped the money.

"That's almost $15,000," he added.

Chasey thought her heart stopped for a second. "We could go and get a start somewhere. Anywhere, Blue-Eyes. Think about it. Take your time. We have a job to finish first."

The Gypsy nodded after she said "anywhere," but he responded, "Okay." Just in case she needed some clarification.

"Let's get to breakin' down this old thing," he said as he jerked his thumb toward the old steam shovel. "While we're doin' it, we can discuss the logistics of where to stage the new stuff and where we might go." He finished up with a smile that melted the chill from the desert night air that started to wrap its arms around Chasey. His smile caused her to run to him and wrap her arms around *him*. She squeezed him a little too tightly again. He grimaced slightly from the pain.

Chasey realized what she did again and released her python-like grasp. She begged, "Oh, Blue-Eyes, I'm so sorry. Please forgive me."

"It's all right. Let me go take some of my 'meds' and we'll get to work. Okay?" Then he kissed her on the nose and started toward the house.

Chasey called out and stopped him. "Hold up, baby," she said as she started after him.

"What?" he asked as he turned around to meet her.

Chasey looked at him sheepishly. She thought carefully about how best to suggest he stop using heroin and try other treatment options. She began slowly, "Have you ever tried any alternative treatments for your pain? I'm not talking tin foil hats and underwear covered in mayo. I'm talking acupressure, yoga, Ayurvedic, and Panchakarma."

"Gesundheit!"

"Smart-ass! Would you be serious for a minute?" she scolded as she smiled and patted him gently on his chest.

He leaned his head down toward hers and gave her a pouty smile of conformance.

After she had his attention, she continued, "This is important. It could mean not having to use the heroin anymore if any of it were to work for you. It's worked for a lot of people in your situation. We can talk about it later when we have time."

"No, now's fine. If it won't take long to do, just do it."

"Some things don't take very long. Some things are lifestyle changes, so they will be things we'll have to talk about over time. Depending on what 'exactly' is wrong with you, I might not be able to help you. You very well may need an operation to correct an old injury that was never properly repaired or even diagnosed."

The Gypsy listened intently to what she told him. Fortunately, or not, he knew what his ailments were.

"I know exactly what's wrong. L3 and L4 are in chronic degeneration. That's allowed arthritis to set in," he told her with confidence. "Plus arthritic knees and hips. I've also got a bad shoulder from an old war injury. And the ribs on the left side that were broken in the accident hurt when it rains along with EVERYTHING else in my body." He continued with a laugh and a smile.

"A lot of it sounds like 'maintenance' stuff to me. Things that can be managed with dietary adjustments like removing pain triggers. Corn and vegetable oils have been linked to joint pain and inflammation. And there is 'pork-induced gout,' so if you eliminate those from your diet, you will eventually gain benefit. But that takes a little time. For something that can work quicker, we can try cold, heat, and this," Chasey handed him a six-inch diameter, eighteen-inch-long foam cylinder.

He looked at it eyes wide and asked, "What the Hello Kitty is this? A suppository?"

"I know you're a bit of an ol' whore, Blue-Eyes," Chasey commented. "But… come on!" she exclaimed as she looked around at his butt and then back at the foam roller. "No, dummy," she continued after she took it back from him and swatted him on his butt. "They are also used for myofascial release."

"Oh, ho ho. That really explained it."

"You lay on it and roll. It decompresses your spine and massages your muscles, in simplest terms," Chasey said with a crinkled nose while she tweaked the Gypsy's nose.

She tossed it on the floor of the room and said, "Sit down on the chair, and then I'll help you get on the floor. Before we start, this will probably hurt and be difficult until you're able relax your back muscles. Who knows how long that will take. Okay?"

"Great," he responded with an abundance of sarcastic exuberance.

"Lay back with the roller at your shoulder, and then lift your butt off the floor. Good. Now, relax your back and let yourself rest. It will take some time. But when it finally happens, it will feel like the foam collapsed."

The Gypsy looked at her with one eye like she had lost her mind.

"No, trust me," she said as she patted him on his chest. "Just wait. When it happens, it will blow your mind. Slowly push with your heels. I'll help support you if you need it. If it starts to hurt as you roll down your back, pull your heels back in and put your butt on the floor."

"Okay," the Gypsy responded skeptically.

As he moved his heels away from his body, the foam roller started to move down his back. He did feel his chest start to open up.

Maybe this wouldn't be too bad after all, he thought. *A little discomfort at the shoulder, but nothing that would make me stop.*

Then he got to the area where his ribs had been broken. As soon as he got to the middle region of his back, he let out a scream that caused Chasey's farm animals to squeal and scatter outside. Chasey, with her arm at the ready under his shoulder, raised him up. His bottom set on the floor with a small thud.

"There. That wasn't so bad now, was it?" she asked with raised eyebrows and a genuine look and tone of concern. "Your back *is* in bad shape. We'll need to start you on a roller table or hydromassage table first."

"I tried a roller table early on and was unable to use it. But that was over twenty years ago," he said. "What's a hydro table?" he asked.

"Hydromassage is like being sprayed with a bunch of water hoses. They're amazing. We'll go into town tomorrow morning and get you a lumbar back brace and see when we can get some time on the tables. I'm a licensed physical therapist," Chasey continued reluctantly. "I have a deal with the local clinic. I do some work for them when they need it, and I get to use the equipment when I need it."

The Gypsy could tell that there was more to the story by her hesitation and decided to prod her for more. "Why don't you do therapy all the time?" he asked.

As she looked up into his big blue eyes, she hoped her next words would not cause him to run away. Chasey had a worried look on her face. She answered with a voice that wavered with fear, "I couldn't handle patients just coming in for pain pills and not even trying to get better. Some of them, you could see in their eyes through the haze that they weren't doing anything at home but taking pain pills. I couldn't do it anymore. I couldn't watch people throw their lives away. Now I only work with people who are willing to help themselves, people who aren't just looking to 'get high.'"

The Gypsy looked down at her as she pressed her head against him and held him. He only had to think for a brief second before he said, "Let's get to work."

They organized and quickly arranged as much of the junk that she already brought home. They took quick inventory of what they needed to do in the morning before they went to the clinic.

When they finished, they went in, cleaned up, and went to bed. Before going to sleep, Chasey asked, "If we leave here, where do you want to go?"

"Somewhere quiet with few people. I like what you have here, if it were a little more wooded."

Chasey tucked herself in front of him where he lay in the bed and said, "Okay."

24

Chasey and the Gypsy finished up at the clinic just after noon. Just as Chasey thought, they were only able to get X-rays, the MRI, and let the doctor on staff there give him a once-over. He, of course, commented on the needle marks. And Chasey quickly came to the Gypsy's defense.

"That's why we're here, Tom. He's not a heavy user. He graduated from morphine to heroin for 'pain treatment' and management."

"When was the last time you used?" Dr. Michaels asked the Gypsy.

"Three or four days. I don't remember."

"How does it make you feel to be without it?"

"Are you a shrink?" the Gypsy asked curtly. He began to get a little annoyed with the doctor's line of questioning.

"Blue-Eyes!" Chasey scolded.

The Gypsy looked slightly toward her and down in obedience like a dog scolded.

As she explained the doctor's line of questioning, she gently patted his arm. "They're standard questions for people who use opioids and illegal drugs to treat pain," Chasey said in her soothing tone. "It's to determine if you would benefit from counseling while coming off the drugs. Some people have trouble letting go of the drug even after getting everything fixed and the pain removed. They've just been so used to the drug that their mind and body don't want to let go. You do not have that problem. That's the least of your problems, old man," she finished with a pat and a smirk.

He looked over at her and gave her that mischievous little boy's grin she had so quickly fallen for those few months ago.

21

Chasey and the Gypsy got up early, fed the animals and did their morning chores, after which they prepared a light breakfast and discussed the morning's plans.

"After we get the teardown started on the shovel and start getting things moved around for the drills, I'll call Nickie and see if she wants to meet us for lunch in town after we get finished at the clinic with your physical therapy. I'm going to have their radiologist give you a full workup so we'll know what's up in case there's something going on you're not aware of, 'kay?" Chasey started.

"You're the boss," he answered tentatively.

"What's wrong?"

He looked up from picking at his eggs and tried to answer but found he was unable to form any words.

Chasey got up and moved around to his side of the table and sat down in his lap. She held his head close and tight against her chest and said, "I'll be with you the whole time."

"Okay," was all he managed to say after a brief pause.

22

Chasey and the Gypsy finished arranging things and started the break down the old steam shovel. When they came to a point where they could easily stop, Chasey decided they should get ready to go to town. They cleaned up and readied themselves to go to the clinic. While the Gypsy cleaned up, Chasey called Nickie.

"Hey, Nickie. Blue-Eyes and I are going to go to the clinic, and I'm going to check him out and start some PT on him. You want to meet us for lunch after? I've got a *big* job lined up, and we could use your help."

"Sure thing. I've not got much going on that I can't put on hold. What time and where for lunch?" Nickie asked excitedly. She was happy to have the opportunity to work with them.

"We'll have to play it by ear. As soon as we get ready, we're heading to the clinic. I'm going to have him x-rayed and MRI'd. Once I get the results, I'll be able to get a course of treatment planned out for him and hopefully get him off the heroin. To be honest, I don't think it's going to be that difficult. He hasn't used any in a couple of days that I know of."

"I think he uses it mostly out of boredom and habit than pain now."

"I do too," Chasey agreed.

"I'll get cleaned up after I finish what I've got going. When you get ready to go and eat, give me a call."

"Okay. Thanks, Nickie. Bye."

"Bye, Chasey."

23

Chasey and the Gypsy finished getting cleaned up and loaded up in the old Dodge. The Gypsy backed the truck out of the drive, and they headed into town to the physical therapy clinic. On the way, Chasey tried to comfort the Gypsy. She explained what the doctors were going to do to him. And if they had time, what PT she would try to do with him today.

"We probably won't get much more done today than your tests and a good exam. So tomorrow we'll start actually doing work. I want to start you off on the hydromassage table and then use heat and estim."

"What's 'estim'?" the Gypsy asked.

"Electrical stimulation therapy. It's used to treat muscle spasms and pain. It can also be used to exercise muscles gently like a damaged lower back. That way you're able to strengthen your muscles without risking damaging the back. I have a portable TENS unit at home."

"What, you just stick a wire in the wall and make me stand in some water?" he asked in his usual smart-ass tone. Chasey gave him *her* usual look when he made such inquiries or statements. To apologize, the Gypsy wrapped his arm around her, pulled her in tight and kissed the top of her head.

He was only able to maintain the embrace briefly as they approached the turnoff to the clinic because he needed both hands on the steering wheel to turn the old Dodge. It had '39 Dodge power steering. It took "all the power" you could muster up to turn it.

The clinic was a left off the main street and only a block up from the bar where the two of them met.

No wonder Rachael and Chasey were always at each other's throats. They saw each other every day if they were both working here then, he thought as he pulled into the parking lot.

24

Chasey and the Gypsy finished up at the clinic just after noon. Just as Chasey thought, they were only able to get X-rays, the MRI, and let the doctor on staff there give him a once-over. He, of course, commented on the needle marks. And Chasey quickly came to the Gypsy's defense.

"That's why we're here, Tom. He's not a heavy user. He graduated from morphine to heroin for 'pain treatment' and management."

"When was the last time you used?" Dr. Michaels asked the Gypsy.

"Three or four days. I don't remember."

"How does it make you feel to be without it?"

"Are you a shrink?" the Gypsy asked curtly. He began to get a little annoyed with the doctor's line of questioning.

"Blue-Eyes!" Chasey scolded.

The Gypsy looked slightly toward her and down in obedience like a dog scolded.

As she explained the doctor's line of questioning, she gently patted his arm. "They're standard questions for people who use opioids and illegal drugs to treat pain," Chasey said in her soothing tone. "It's to determine if you would benefit from counseling while coming off the drugs. Some people have trouble letting go of the drug even after getting everything fixed and the pain removed. They've just been so used to the drug that their mind and body don't want to let go. You do not have that problem. That's the least of your problems, old man," she finished with a pat and a smirk.

He looked over at her and gave her that mischievous little boy's grin she had so quickly fallen for those few months ago.

25

After they finished with the doctor at the clinic, they scheduled an appoitment for the Gypsy to start his first PT session at ten the next morning. When Chasey finished with the check out nurse, she called Nickie and invited her to join them at the café a couple of blocks past *Rachael's* bar. Nickie said she was ready and on her way.

Chasey hung up the phone at the clinic, turned to the Gypsy and asked, "Want to just walk? We've got the time."

"Sure."

As they approached the parking lot just before the bar, it occurred to the Gypsy where they were. Because of her history with the barmaid, he asked of Chasey in his best sarcastic voice with one eyebrow raised, "Don't chew tink we ought to cross da road here, Miss Chasey?"

Chasey let go of the arm she held and placed both hands on her hips. She gave him an evil look, and shot back, "No, just ME! You can stay here by yourself, and I'll walk over there by myself." She stomped her way across the road to the other side.

The Gypsy watched her every stomp. He thought, *She's even trying to shake her butt extra hard on purpose.* It caused him to laugh out loud. Chasey threw an angry, seductive glance over her shoulder.

After she reached the other side, they both walked in the direction of the restaurant. They tried to watch each other as best they could without falling down or running into something.

When they came to the spot where they first saw each other, they both stopped. Almost instinctively. They stood there and looked at each other.

The Gypsy looked back across the street where his relationship with Chasey began those short months ago before they decided to leave this little town that she spent her entire life in and start a new one together. He considered how things might have been different if he had taken up the Twink on his offer first. Then came the last clear vision the Gypsy would have for a very long time, if ever.

The sound of the blaring semitruck air horn, screeching tires, breaking glass, and bending metal was deafening. The last sight he saw of Chasey was of her as she looked in the direction of the deafening noise. Then a jackknifed semitruck with trailer and a small pickup skidded by. They produced a huge cloud of smoke and dust as they passed. After the Gypsy stopped blinking, he adjusted his mind to what happened and realized that people were running past where Chasey once stood. The barmaid and Jeb came up to the Gypsy and spoke to him, but he was unable to hear anything.

With a twitch of his body, the Gypsy was finally able to bring himself to utter, "I have to go." He turned around and walked into the desert past the bar in which he spent so much time and become fond of a great many people. The barmaid and Jeb knew better than to try to follow him, and they also knew they would never see the Gypsy again.

PART II

THE BODY HOLDS STRONG

1

"I need three units of blood! Get a clamp on that bleeder in her leg!"

"There's too much damage here, Doctor."

"Don't talk, work! We'll deal with the extremities later! Move, people!"

"I lost the pulse, Doctor!"

2

Taylor found the Gypsy facedown in the truck stop bathroom toilet. He found his brothers like this before and hated it more every time. Taylor helped the Gypsy up off the floor. He washed him a little and then flushed his "stuff." That was when he noticed the Gypsy's eyes and looked away.

A look too long into "those eyes" might prove fatal, Taylor thought.

"Leave me," the Gypsy commanded weakly from the floor.

"Nah," Taylor responded as he had many times before to the same command. "Let's grab a cup and a bagel instead." He extended his hand down to the Gypsy, who still had not managed to find his feet.

Eventually, the Gypsy pulled himself up off the floor of the truck stop bathroom, with Taylor's help. *Why won't he just leave me? It would be better,* the Gypsy thought as he tried to steady himself while he leaned against the sink. *But why did he have to flush my "meds"?* If the Gypsy could ever think clearly and speak again, he would have to try to remember to ask him.

Taylor helped him outside into the early-morning sunlight. They went across the street to a tree with some grass that the Gypsy could lay on and rest while Taylor went into the diner and bought them some breakfast. While Taylor was inside, the Gypsy tried to remember how much time passed since he lost Chasey. He thought, two, maybe three months, since he left that cursed town. But his perceptions were muddled because of his drug-induced state. He started to cry but banged his head against the tree to keep himself from doing so.

The place that taught him you could have a life of love without sex was the same place that took it all away from him. His face contorted into a cruel snarl as he thought, *Maybe I should go back and burn it down. That would show that damn, good-for-nothing town.* And then he threw up.

Taylor found the Gypsy where he had left him outside the truck stop, under a shade tree (like he had been capable of going anywhere). He handed the Gypsy the cup of coffee and a plain bagel. Taylor doubted very seriously he would be able to keep very much of either of them down. A sip of coffee, a bite of bagel, a chew, a swallow, and not even five seconds, back up it all came.

Taylor convinced the Gypsy to come back to his home with him and at least clean himself before he "continued his journey." Reluctantly and very slowly, the Gypsy got to his feet with Taylor's assistance and they started the short walk to Taylor's place of residence.

3

Chasey could see the Gypsy's smile and "those eyes" from across the street. The same street she caught him staring at her can not so long ago. Now she was leaving to start a new life with him. Who would have thought. The same "dirty ol' man" she caught staring at her can and practically drooling on himself, she was now leaving to start a life with him. The same man that entered the town a drug-abusing prostitute...

Those eyes were all she "could" see. Just the blue, in fact. And the *pain*! "Make the PAIN GO AWAY, Blue-Eyes!" Chasey screamed. But she could not hear herself. Why? The *pain*! And then the blackness came.

4

Nickie walked into the bar. She slowly walked up to the spot a couple of places down from where Jeb rested his elbows and hung his head low. As she hit the bar, dressed all in black, she flung one leg up on the footrest. She looked over at Jeb and made eye contact with him for the first time since she walked into the room. He nodded hi to her and went back to letting his head hang down.

"Has anybody seen or heard ANYTHING about Blue-Eyes?" Nickie implored the barmaid.

From her perch on the cooler, as she exhaled her most recent puff off her cigarette, she slowly shook her head no. With that, Nickie joined Jeb in hanging his head.

5

Taylor and the Gypsy arrived at his place about an hour after they started. It was normally a ten-minute walk for Taylor, but today he had to make several stops to wait on the Gypsy to recover so he was able to continue. They eventually made it there, and Taylor got him inside. As he helped him inside, Taylor tried to imagine what his story might be. He was sure it was a broken heart caused by a woman somehow. There is *always* a woman involved. Even if it's a *he*. Taylor had his heart broken a time or two by the likes of the Gypsy, so he knew he had to be careful. He had a glimpse into "those eyes" once already. He knew he would have to be *very* careful.

Taylor finished helping the Gypsy clean up and wrapped him in a towel while his clothes washed. Taylor convinced him to stay long enough to let him clean his clothes. At least that was some progress. Maybe he could save this one.

Taylor told the Gypsy as he sat him on the couch, "I have to go to work. Stay here and eat some more bagel and drink some more water."

"Yes, Mom," the Gypsy snorted back as Taylor headed out the door.

Before he shut and locked the door, Taylor called back, "There's some fruit in the fridge."

Had the Gypsy the strength, he would have given Taylor the single-finger salute for that remark. *Why is he mother-henning me?* The Gypsy thought as he started to drift off. *Why didn't he just leave me?*

"Oh, Chasey!" the Gypsy screamed. And then he cried himself to sleep.

6

"How are her vitals, nurse?"

"Stable for now, Doctor."

"Keep a close eye on her, nurse. She has a long way to go before we can even begin to reconstruct her arm and leg."

"Will she ever walk again?"

"Maybe… But she will probably never see out of her left eye… or have hearing in the left ear…"

7

Taylor got back from work a few hours before dawn. He found the Gypsy sitting in the corner half asleep. He started cleaning up after work. Most nights it was clean work, but then there were nights like tonight where you come home covered in crap from head to toe. He did not mind waiting tables. He always liked to meet new people. While the pay was better before he was forced to buy insurance he still made a decent wage.

Taylor would supplement his income with odd jobs at the local bail bonds. His ability and likability made him an easy person with whom to talk and afforded him the good fortune of being able to find bond jumpers. Plus, he had a lot of experience with tracking from hunting as a child and being a scout when he was in the military.

A couple of days passed, and one night after Taylor got cleaned up and caught a couple of hours' sleep, the phone rang. It woke him quickly as it always did. It was the bondsman. He needed him to track a "jumper." He got the Gypsy up, fed him a little, and suggested he take a shower while he cleaned up the dishes.

The Gypsy enjoyed his shower. The first time in a while. He let the water hit the top of his head and run down his shoulders and his back. He thought about smiling. The first time in a while. And Taylor was the reason why.

Taylor came into the bathroom and said, "The call I got was work. They need me to come in." He stuck his head in the shower. "Mind if I join you?" he asked playfully.

The Gypsy huffed and then answered, "Okay." He stepped forward so Taylor could get wet and soap up. Taylor stood there and soaped up while the water washed down between the two of them like a shield. The Gypsy thought about how much Taylor helped him get cleaned up while he was here.

He thought about why he was so messed up in the first place. That made the happiness he started to feel fade. That was the first time he started to feel anything other than pain since…

The Gypsy hung his head as he faced the wall. Taylor sensed something was wrong. They were together for only a short time, but he could always *sense* when a ghost from the Gypsy's past bothered him.

"Are you all right?" Taylor asked, as he touched his shoulder. He tried to be as comforting as he could.

The Gypsy gave him a shrug and a sideways nod as to indicate, "What do you think?"

"Would you like for me to wash your back before I leave?"

The Gypsy hesitated for a second and then nodded yes.

8

Nickie was at Chasey's side when she first opened her eye. Three days passed since Chasey's eyes were closed. Nickie visited her every day while she waited for her to regain consciousness. If she was not at the hospital or working, she tried to find the Gypsy. Nickie hoped she would be able to find him before Chasey opened her eyes. She had not had any luck in that department yet. Chasey needed to have him by her side to help her with the long road of rehab she had ahead of her.

Chasey looked around while she tried to get her bearings on where she was. She tried to process what happened to her, but most importantly...

Chasey started to get a little agitated when she could not find the Gypsy. Nickie noticed her struggling.

She reached out, grabbed her gently to calm her down, and said, "He's not here, Chasey. I'm not sure where he is either."

Chasey looked up at Nickie with concern.

"We've been looking," Nickie said flatly as she started to cry. "They... they couldn't find you for a while after the semitruck clipped you." Nickie stopped and swallowed hard. She wiped away some tears before she continued. "People were screaming 'She's gone! SHE'S GONE!' and I know that was the last thing Blue-Eyes heard and thought the worst." Nickie paused for a moment. A tear rolled down what was exposed of Chasey's right cheek from the bandages to her head wounds. Nickie wiped it away with a gentle sweep of her finger.

Nickie continued, "They found your body in the lobby of the bookstore. You were under a bookshelf and display stand."

"Wow," Chasey managed with a slight chuckle. "What's the tally?" She motioned at her body with a weak sweep of her finger.

Nickie struggled with what she should tell her. She eventually managed to start and said, "Your left leg was broken in sixteen places." The femur is in eight itself. The right has two breaks and a couple of minor fractures and some knee damage. Your pelvis is broken. Six ribs are fractured or broken. Your left arm was almost severed from your body. It was terribly dislocated. You have a severe concussion. The damage to you left ear is so bad you will probably have permanent hearing loss. They're not sure about your left eye. You almost lost it. You also had a collapsed lung. And last but not least…" Nickie tried to add with a little fanfare, "a bruised kidney. So if you see a little blood in your pee, you'll know why." Nickie then laid her head down on Chasey's arm and cried.

"Wow" was all Chasey was able to manage. Not even a chuckle. She was barely even able to manage a breath. Then she asked Nickie, "Please don't stop looking for Blue-Eyes."

"I won't. Rachael has her connections checking everywhere too."

Chasey looked off across the room when Nickie told her. Her breath almost left her. *Is that whore going to try to get Blue-Eyes for herself now that I'm 'out-of-the-picture' as it were?* she thought.

Nickie looked up at Chasey. She noticed she started to get a little worked up and realized why. "For YOU, Chasey! She's looking for HIM FOR YOU!" Nickie almost yelled. She fought the urge she had to shake Chasey as she placed her hands on her shoulders.

"Chasey, Rachael really is upset about how everything wound up between the two of you," she said more calmly as she sat back. "I know there can never be anything between the two of you, but know this, she is NOT going to do ANYTHING to come between you and Blue-Eyes. She regrets losing his friendship. Even beyond losing the benefits, she regrets losing his friendship the most."

"Thank you, Nickie. You always have been my best friend."

9

After Taylor finished washing the Gypsy's broad, slightly muscular back, the Gypsy turned to face Taylor. Taylor stepped closer to him.

"I need to go. Will you be all right?" he asked.

The Gypsy nodded.

Taylor kissed him and got out of the shower. He dried off and dressed for work. While he did, the Gypsy let the shower massage beat on his sore joints, muscles, and bones. What was it she had told him?

"Keep moving. Move every day." *She was always right.* He thought, *And DAMN IT! Taylor's doing the same thing.* How long had he been here? It turned out to have been less than a week instead of months, but still, *Too long,* he thought.

"I'm going," Taylor called out from the other room as he headed out for work. "I'm not sure when I'll be back since I wasn't even supposed to work today."

Taylor never saw the Gypsy again.

10

Nickie and Chasey spent most of the evening reminiscing about all the things they scavenged together and recycled. They discussed the pink rat rod Jeep they built together for most of the time Nickie was there with Chasey.

"Those were the best times," Nickie said as she patted Chasey's hand lightly. "You look like you need you get some sleep."

Nickie got up and kissed Chasey on what was left exposed of her right forehead from bandages and said, "Try to rest. EVERYONE is looking for Blue-Eyes. I'm going to go check a couple of places after I grab a bite and check in with Rachael."

"Thank you, Nickie. Be careful. You know those places can be dangerous," Chasey responded with a worried look.

Nickie waved as she walked out the door, then Chasey called out to her, "Thank Rachael for her help for me, will you."

Nickie stuck her head back in the doorway and said with a loving smile, "Sure thing. I'll see you tomorrow," and then she left for the night.

Chasey closed her eye and tried to sleep, but all she did was think about the Gypsy. She hoped Nickie would find him soon and find him safe. Chasey had troubling dreams all night. She dreamed about every imaginable situation in which the Gypsy could wind up in trouble or worse. It was the worst that always jolted her out of any semblance of sleep she found.

Every time Chasey woke up she tried to reassure herself that everything was alright. She needed her sleep and rest because she had a long road to recovery. Also, Nickie looked for the Gypsy every chance she had. Her assurances never seemed to amount to much. She chuckled a little at the thought.

"Oh, God," Chasey called out, "I know we don't talk much, but would you keep Blue-Eyes safe until I can find him if Nickie can't."

For whatever reason, Chasey was able to close her eyes and sleep peacefully for a couple of hours until sunrise.

11

The nurse woke Chasey as she checked her bandages. Chasey asked, "How's it look?"

Helen knew Chasey's sense of humor. She replied, "It doesn't look any worse than it did when you came in here. I guess that's something," she added with a wink and a smile. "Were you able to get any rest?"

"A little. I can't stop worrying about Blue-Eyes," Chasey replied as Helen held her hand to try to comfort her. "I hope Nickie finds him soon."

As Helen started to leave to continue her rounds, she said, "I know you'll get tired of hearing this, but try to get some rest. I'll check back in with you after I finish my morning rounds before the doctor gets here."

"Okay" was all Chasey said.

She did not even look her way. Chasey was either thinking about the Gypsy or in the beginning of getting her rehabilitation and physical therapy plan of action ready. All she needed to know was when she would be able to get out of the hospital. *And they better not give me any of that "You have to wait until you have completely healed" bullshit they tell the other patients,* Chasey thought.

Chasey always told her patients the same thing. She had things to do and did not have time to "completely heal." As soon as the stitches could come out, work would begin. Maybe sooner.

Chasey grimaced in pain as she tried to lift her "good-enough" leg. She needed to assess the damage. She wanted to find out what she would be able to do while immobile. As the doctor came into the room early to pay her a surprise visit, she thought out loud, "Definitely sooner."

"What's 'definitely sooner'?" the doctor asked as he entered the room and saw Chasey's leg drop from being lifted just barely an inch. "I wouldn't be trying to move too much just yet, young lady. I know how stubborn you are, Chasey. But this is one time you will have to wait just a little while to let yourself heal before you can get started. For a normal person, I would say a month," he said. He held her HAND FIRMLY, leaned in closely, and looked right into her one eye that did not have a bandage. He added while he maintained his firm grip and piercing stare, "For you, three weeks, minimum! If you do not wait, you WILL NOT recover."

Chasey let out an exhale of air from her nose in disgust as she turned her head to avoid his gaze and to let the doctor know she had no intention of doing any such thing.

The doctor gently grabbed Chasey's chin with his finger and turned her to look his direction so she could see and hear him and said, "If I have to, Chasey, I'll chain you to this bed. I may have lost you as my love, but I will not let you lose your life. All your friends are looking for him. As soon as you are ready, you can go. Okay? Don't make me tie you up."

Chasey looked at him with as crooked a look as she could through all her bandages and said, "You'd like that just a little too much, wouldn't you... Jeremy?"

"Don't call me that!" he said seethingly through his teeth. He huffed, left her side, and headed toward the doorway of Chasey's room where he paused. Without turning, he added, "Please rest." He managed calmly, "I'll check on you before I leave tonight." He left her room and turned down the hall to continue his morning rounds.

As soon as he turned the corner, Chasey gritted her teeth and lifted her leg again.

12

Dr. Paulson paused outside his next patient's room and leaned against the wall by the door to compose himself after his and Chasey's "morning checkup." She was always confrontational and lashed out when she was in pain, either physical or emotional. And she was hurting both ways. And just about as bad as could possibly be imagined.

The two of them grew up together. They first met in grade school. As long as Dr. Paulson was able to remember, Chasey was a stubborn, hardheaded, and headstrong person. Especially when it came to taking care of herself. No one could ever tell Ms. Chasey MacDonald what to do.

"Only time will tell," Dr. Paulson said under his breath. Only time would tell if Chasey would let herself heal or if she would tear herself apart in haste to find the one she loved.

He shook his head, took a deep breath, put on his best smile, and went into the next room.

"Good morning, Mrs. Simpson. And how are we feeling this morning?"

13

Chasey lay in her bed. She looked at the ceiling with her eye as she mulled over what Dr. Paulson told her. Her leg and abdomen throbbed in pain from where she lifted her leg.

Was he right? she thought. *Did I always push myself too hard?* The pain in her stitching told her a resounding yes.

She knew she would be of no use to the Gypsy unless she was as close to one hundred percent as she could possibly get. And she would not be able to do that as soon as possible unless she let herself heal first.

She closed her eye and let herself think about when she and Andrew Paulson grew up together. He always loved her. In her own way, she still loved him. Just not in the way he wanted her to love him. He wanted a trophy wife. But that was no*t t*he life she wanted then or even wanted now.

Chasey was still too strong-willed to be "restrained," "civilized," or "broken." Those were the words she used when Andy brought up marriage when they dated. They always made him laugh. He always insisted he just wanted to make an "honest" woman out of her.

"What the HELL was that supposed to mean, anyway?" she asked out loud. She surprised herself that she said it aloud.

As she lay there in bed, Chasey thought back to when she grew up with Andy before he "got in trouble" and was "sent away." Back then he was the shy little bookworm of a kid who liked to dissect worms, crayfish, frogs, and whatever else he caught in the local stream. That led to the usual bullying.

Eventually, Andy took all the name-calling and abuse he could tolerate, and he snapped. There were four of them and only Andy. The exact details of what Andy did to the four boys were never made public, and to this day he never told Chasey. It must have been bad because she remembered that those boys were not seen for almost a year, and one of them never returned to town.

It always bothered her how everyone treated the bullies as the victims when the person who received the bullying snapped. It was always the same excuses, "Boys will be boys," or "It's good for them. It will toughen them up."

"Bullshit!" Chasey thought out loud.

Chasey and Andy dated while they were in high school after he came back from his "rest". Every time he did something that irritated her, she called him Jeremy, like in the song of the same name by Pearl Jam. That always sent him into a fit and end the argument with a win for her. A little childish, sure, but no more so than what he did. He always wanted to dress her up and parade her around like some trophy wife and keep her on a pedestal!

14

It took Chasey just over two weeks to get well enough to where the hospital was willing to let her go home without fear of any liability on their part. She was caught a couple of times as she tried to escape, already. She was caught the first time when she poured herself into a wheelchair just eight days after the wreck. One of the nurses intercepted her as she headed toward the door. On day twelve, the hospital security guard escorted her back in on the mop handle she used as a crutch.

Dr. Paulson had Nickie aside while Chasey signed her release paperwork and pleaded, "Don't let her kill herself over that crazy old man."

Nickie just stared blankly back at him.

"Please!" he begged.

"I never understood what she saw in you. Blue-Eyes treats her ten times as good as you ever believe you did, could, or would!" Nickie responded. She poked him in his chest to emphasize her point that she would in no way he*lp* him.

Dr. Paulson hung his head and walked away.

Nickie never liked Andy. He always held the fact he was bullied over everyone's heads. Like *he* was the only one to get bullied and snap. The stories *she* could tell *him*.

Nickie shook her head and composed herself as Chasey finished filling out the last of the papers for her release from the hospital. Nickie dreaded telling her that she did not have any news at all of the Gypsy.

Nickie pushed Chasey out of the hospital toward the town car she rented to take her home. She knew when Chasey looked up at her that she waited for the information about the Gypsy Nickie lacked.

Nickie loaded Chasey into the car in silence. She tried to avoid eye contact with her as much as possible.

After Nickie pointed the town car down the road toward Chasey's house, she could no longer stand her stare. Nickie finally spoke, "We've looked EVERYWHERE! It's like he just walked into the desert and vanished." Nickie pulled over because she knew she would not be able to continue to drive while they talked about him.

Chasey stopped giving Nickie a death stare and looked at her hands and then her leg. *It still needs a lot of rehab,* she thought.

Nickie continued after a brief pause, "We've even hired trackers to take the same path that Rachael and Jeb saw Blue-Eyes take into the desert."

When Chasey heard Rachael's name a look of complete and total evil came over her face. She slowly raised her head and turned it toward Nickie as her heart filled with hate.

Nickie saw the look that came over Chasey and saw the hate within her eyes. She saw that hatred once before in Chasey. It was for her sister, Rachael. Nickie realized what thought consumed Chasey, and she screamed, "No! Chasey, NO!"

Nickie reached over and gently grabbed Chasey so she could turn her to face her. She did not want to risk doing her any harm or cause her any pain. Nickie intended to make *damn* sure she heard her. She was putting an end to this schoolgirl jealous feud once and for all before it killed all of them!

"Damn it, Chasey!" she screamed. "Rachael is not trying to derail your life," she added as she slowly squeezed Chasey until she grimaced. The mild pain snapped her out of her rage.

Nickie kissed her on her forehead and sat back into the driver's seat. She took a few loud, deep breaths while she thought about how best to continue. While she did, Chasey settled herself back into her seat and sat in silence with her chin on her chest.

Nickie finally spoke, "You have to believe me, Chasey. Rachael's the one who hired the people to track Blue-Eyes. And *not* to find him for herself. I know you may find it difficult to believe, but she has changed since you and Blue-Eyes settled down together. After he and Rachael had their big blowup, Jeb and her had a long talk, and she has settled down quite a bit. I'm not sure what Jeb said to her. Whatever it was, it worked."

Chasey turned her head toward Nickie so she was able to hear her better so Nickie would not need to shout. Nickie's voice cracked just a little more than usual because she spoke a little louder due to Chasey's loss of hearing in her left ear.

After Chasey looked in Nickie's direction, Nickie continued in a quieter and more comfortable voice, "She's actually happy. She's stopped drinking… heavily," she said with a chuckle. "And she even closes the bar and goes to bed and sleeps a decent night's sleep for once in her life. She's NEVER done that as long as I've known her. She's always been a vampire. You know that."

Chasey looked at Nickie with a wide-eyed stare of complete disbelief and shock. She looked down and spoke, slowly and softly, "I'm sorry, Nickie. It's… just… we've had such bad blood between us. All I think about when I hear any mention of her is what happened to Michael."

"You can't lay all the blame on Rachael, Chasey."

"I know, Nickie. I'm sorry. But he didn't have to kill himself!"

"He had other things bothering him. You even said that he was showing signs of troubles yourself, and no one listened. Remember?"

Chasey closed her eyes and nodded. She opened them and said, "You're right. I'm sorry. Let's go home. I've got work to do."

"You've got to rest first."

"We'll see about that," Chasey mumbled under her breath as she turned back to face the front window.

"What?"

"Huh? Oh, nothing. Just thinking out loud."

Nickie was fairly certain she heard what she said. She decided right then and there she was going to have to stay with her for a little while just to make sure she didn't kill herself before she got well enough to go find the Gypsy.

15

It took Chasey barely six months to get herself back to the edge of the road where it all began. Where she first felt his stare. Where she first looked into "those eyes." All those firsts. And where she last saw him before the darkness took him from her. Six months of pain, suffering, and emptiness. Now she had to find him and set the world right again.

She used her hands on her knee to assist her as she stood. She pushed herself up with her good leg from where she kneeled to study the terrain. Rachael, Jeb, and Nickie stood behind her. They watched her intently and said nothing. They all learned a long time ago not to interrupt her when she was in deep concentration.

Nickie stepped forward after Chasey stood and spoke first, "It's been a long time. Who knows where he is or what kind of shape he's in. Don't be away too long."

"I will find him" was all Chasey said.

After Chasey hugged Nickie, she turned and walked off into the desert. She followed the path Rachael and Jeb told her they saw the Gypsy take.

PART III

THE SOUL WINS IN THE END

1

When Chasey finally caught up to the Gypsy, she found him with a needle in his arm. The only way she even knew it was him was by "those eyes." In the condition he was in, the Gypsy was not sure if what he saw was real or not when he saw her.

As she came closer, he tried to ask, "Chasey?" before his "meds" took him into the darkness for what Chasey hoped would be the last time but not the *last* time. She bent down, removed the syringe from his arm and the rubber hose he had tied off around his arm, and picked him up. She was able to carry him; there was so little left of him. That would not have been possible when they met those eighteen months ago.

Chasey loaded the Gypsy in the old Dodge and took him to the only place she knew she would be able to get him the help he would need. But it was the one place the Gypsy swore he would *never* go back. The VA.

All of Chasey's scars from the wreck were not as visible as was her love for the Gypsy. The hospital staff at the VA told her she had to leave the room while they tended to the Gypsy. When she refused, they did not bother to ask again. Chasey's main concern was how mad the Gypsy would be when he found out that he was at the VA. She remembered how much he hated the Veterans' Administration. He always complained about how they screwed up everything, if they ever *did* anything. Supposedly, there were big changes in the way the VA worked now. Only time would be able to tell if they could heal these wounds.

The Gypsy did not talk about most of his time in the service after his injuries. That's where it seemed the problems began to arise.

And Chasey never pressed him. But when he did talk, it was always of broken promises and of the fact that they did not fix anything.

The Gypsy opened his eyes to see Chasey. She looked down into "those eyes" with genuine concern.

"You were gone," he managed weakly as tears formed across his eyes.

His eyes veered over to the left side of her face and saw the scarring. He started to have an emotional fit as he reached his hand toward her left cheek. He tried to say he was sorry but was unable to get any air into his lungs. He only managed a couple of squeaks before he started to choke.

Chasey saw him begin to struggle, both physically and emotionally. She reached out and took him by the hand he tried to use to touch her cheek and held it close to her chest.

"No," she said firmly. "Don't think about it right now. Let's just concentrate on getting you better. Okay? I love you. And we're together. That's all that matters. Now, rest."

She placed his hand on his chest and patted him as she had so many times before to calm him. And as it had so many times before, it calmed him almost instantly. Chasey knew he would need his physical strength before they could begin to start on the emotional healing from what happened the day she was hit by the semitruck.

2

Recovery from addiction for some can take a long time and can be a lifelong struggle. But luckily for the Gypsy, he had no reason nor desire to use his "meds" anymore, so his recovery was more dependency and just getting his health back from the ravages of the demon that is heroin. He also had Chasey. He would spend the rest of his life with her while he made amends for how he turned his back on her. Even if it killed him. So it was not much of a surprise that his recovery was as quick as it was.

The Gypsy's stay at the VA hospital was brief. He probably left before he was completely physically ready. By the time they walked out of the door of the VA hospital, the Gypsy and Chasey put away the ugliness that happened. And they never spoke of it again. It was almost two years since Chasey was hit by the semitruck, so they decided they would start living their lives together from today.

3

Several years passed since Chasey found the Gypsy in the cardboard drug den. It was time he made a commitment to her. It was quite obvious to the Gypsy that she was totally committed to him. The only thing he had left that he considered valuable, other than Chasey, was the ring from his military service. Somehow after all the hell he put himself through over the years, he managed to hang on to it. It was 18-carat yellow gold with a large black onyx stone. He couldn't remember the size, if he ever knew. It also had four small rubies surrounded by four diamond chips each at their respective corners of the rubies. He thought he might be able to get an engagement ring made for her from this ring.

The Gypsy saved some money secretly from Chasey so he could get her ring made. He was always concerned she might find out he did not "report" all of his earnings. If she found out, she might think that he secretly drank more than a drink or two a week or that he started using drugs again. She finally got him to stop referring to them as his "meds" last year.

"Duh, Nile isn't just the name of a river in Africa." She drove him crazy with that line. He thought about that as she walked past with the morning animal feed. The Gypsy wondered if maybe it was as much out of her badgering him that he finally stopped calling the heroin his "meds" or not.

"Who cares," he said out loud.

"What'd you say, Blue-Eyes?" Chasey asked back.

"Huh? What? Oh, nothing. Just thinking out loud," he responded with a slight chuckle. "I need to go into town today and, uh, check for... on, on some... thing," he said. He tried not to sound suspicious but failed miserably at it.

Chasey looked at him a little concerned. She was always able to tell when he lied. He hardly ever did. This was not lying. This was something else.

What is going on in his mind? Chasey wondered.

"Okay?" she replied. "Do you want me to go with you?" she asked, to see what his response would be.

"Huh? Oh no. I'll be all right. You've got, uh, you know, those things you're going to be doing later. This shouldn't take long. I'll be right back," the Gypsy finished. He got into their truck and headed toward town to find a jeweler.

As Chasey watched the Gypsy head out of the driveway, she knew he was up to something. It was obvious. She just hoped it was not something "bad." But she *knew* he was up to *something*. She just had to decide on *how* to handle *what* situation might arise and *if* she should try to intervene… and *when*.

4

The Gypsy pulled into the adobe structure–lined streets of town just as the town began to spring to life. There were a lot of artists in this part of town who made jewelry. He should be able to find someone to make a ring for him. He knew of the blacksmith's apprentice who made a lot of jewelry of her own designs. Chasey always commented that she liked her work. The Gypsy thought she would be a good place to start.

The Gypsy pulled into the parking lot and parked next to a very large articulated structure. The local blacksmith Magnus Karlsen worked on it. It was an assembly for either himself or a customer. The Gypsy passed by Magnus. Magnus raised his blond mane–covered head in a nod of recognition to the Gypsy's arrival between strikes on the bar of iron on which he worked. Magnus was a giant Norwegian. He was a mountain of a man at six feet and eight inches and more than four hundred pounds, if there was a scale that could weigh him other than at the stockyards.

Magnus swung that hammer well enough that it made Hephaestus proud. It was a hammer the Gypsy believed he could barely lift much less swing. He swore he felt himself come off the ground a little every time Magnus delivered a blow with that mighty hammer.

The Gypsy threw up his hand as he always did. He passed Magnus and headed back to where the apprentice tended a smaller forge. She was a fuller-figured woman in her early twenties. She had on dungaree tops and bottoms covered with leather chaps and smock. She had hair the color of mud tied up in braids wrapped around her head and covered with a blue bandanna. Kelly was her name. She was a local girl of German stock. She fit her stereotype well. And her jeans as well. She was bent over pumping the bellows. The Gypsy watched the sweat as it ran down the crease of her back into her pants from where she had her top tied up and thought...

The Gypsy shook himself. *Whoa. Old habits...* After he shook the thoughts he had about Kelly, he looked up at the wall at some jeweled bridles, daggers, and swords that hung there on display. He looked at all the work she displayed for customers as he waited for her to finish.

Kelly was aware that someone walked up behind her. As soon as she was able, she turned to see that it was one of her favorite customers.

"Hey, Blue-Eyes!" she called out while he looked at the wall of objets d'art and gilded weapons. He was looking at an overly ornate set of spurs with jeweled rowels when she caught his attention. "What are you planning on using those for?" she asked seductively and playfully. She was well aware of his past. Chasey told her about the Gypsy's previous occupation in private after they became better acquainted.

He gave her a slight sideways glance with a little of a "what a naughty little girl you are" look. "What kind of person would wear those? Or are they just for decoration?"

"You'd be surprised. Usually wannabes with more money than sense."

They both chuckled while the Gypsy looked at the spurs and shook his head.

Kelly asked, "Where's Chasey?"

"She's home working. I have something I need help with. Can I trust you?"

"Sure," Kelly responded uneasily. She was unsure if she was going to be able to keep her word to the Gypsy because of his past. But with everything Chasey told her about him, she hoped she would because she liked them both.

The Gypsy started slowly, "Chasey really likes your work. She has been there for me always, and it's time for me to do the same for her." He paused and took a deep breath. As he did, Kelly's eyes grew wide with anticipation with what she hoped would be his next words.

He looked at the ground of the forge and moved around some of the dirt there with one of his feet. He acted like a bashful child who wanted to ask a cute girl to the homecoming dance. He eventually raised his eyes just enough to look at Kelly and said, "I need to make a ring."

"Yes!" Kelly barked without hesitation. Her response was so quick and loud that it startled him a little.

"Um, okay. I've been keeping a little money from Chasey to help cover it, and I want to use *this* to make it," he said as he presented his old service ring.

"Are you sure you want to make it out of your military ring, Blue-Eyes?"

"She's more important to me than this. I have my memories, such as they are. And I will still have the ring. Just in a slightly different form."

"Okay. What kind of design were you thinking?"

"If you would be able to get a small solitaire diamond and break up the onyx and then use that and the rubies as accents to maybe encrust the ring somehow…" he trailed off to allow her artistic vision to take over because an artist he was not. "You're familiar with what she likes in your work. I'll take whatever advice you offer."

"Okay. I'll make some drawings for you."

"Good. I need to get back. I'm sure she's already suspicious, because I didn't handle it well when I left this morning. I don't like being deceitful with her."

"I'm fairly sure she'll be all right with this little lie after she finds out about it," Kelly said with a wink and a smile.

The Gypsy nodded and smiled. While he still looked down, he said, "I'll come back next week and see what you've come up with, 'kay?"

"Okay. I'm so happy for you, the both of you," she said as she stepped in and gave him a big hug.

The Gypsy held his head up and hugged her back. After they hugged, he walked out of the forge. As the gypsy headed out of the forge, he passed by the giant Norwegian who continued to work on his current project with Thor's hammer. He threw up his hand, and Magnus as he always did in between blows, nodded.

5

Nickie was under the hood of her pink rat rod Jeep. She heard her landline phone ring while she performed some maintenance on it and gave it a little tune-up. There were only two people who had that number and only *one* person who ever used it, and she *never* called unless it was an emergency. She was the type of person who would rather drive for an hour to say hello to someone than pick up the phone and call them. To Nickie's knowledge, she never owned a cell phone. And neither had her "old man."

When Nickie heard the phone, it caused her to drop the wrench she used to remove the valve cover. She needed to get at a lifter that knocked a little. As she climbed down, she bumped the breather and air filter. While she ran to catch the phone, they fell to the ground.

Nickie caught the phone mid-ring. Before she lifted the receiver of the cat-shaped phone (which she painted her favorite color of pink) very far off its resting place, she yelled, "Chasey!"

"Hi, Nickie," Chasey replied with a slight quiver in her voice that was a little unusual for her.

"Wh-what's… wrong?" Nickie started slowly. "How's… everything?… And Blue-Eyes?"

"That's why I'm calling."

Nickie's heart sank. She lost all strength in her legs and sat down hard on the floor. "I'm on my way," she said flatly and placed the receiver back on its base.

She went back outside and finished the tune up on the pink beast and put it back together. After she put the Jeep back together, Nickie quickly packed a few things and took a quick shower. As she ran to the Jeep, she tossed her bag into the back of it and made as much noise as the big block Chevy was able to generate to get to Chasey.

6

The Gypsy sat bolt upright in bed. He more felt it than heard it. His motion roused Chasey from the restless sleep she was having.

"What's wrong?" she asked with genuine concern. She hoped that it was his conscience and that it finally got to him so he would own up to what he did.

"Nickie's on her way. She's almost here," he looked at her and smiled. "Did she let you know she was coming?"

"I called and invited her. It's been a couple of years since I've seen her," she said. She thought about lying briefly, but then thought better of it.

"Good. Me too."

"How do you know she's coming?"

"She's in that rat rod of hers. Can't you FEEL it?"

Chasey gave him one of her "you have got to be out of your mind" looks. And then, she *did* feel it, and her eyes and mouth opened wide in disbelief. She was not sure which of them were more agape, if one were possible to be more so than the other.

"She's coming down the river road now. Approaching the bridge before our turnoff. Wait for it..." The Gypsy made a motion with his finger that coincided with the down shift that proceeded her turn onto their road. Chasey then heard the low guttural rumble of Nickie's rat rod's big block Chevy. "Get dressed."

They both jumped out of bed and threw on their clothes. They got to the front porch in time to see Nickie as she pulled into their drive with the proverbial shit-eatin' grin on her face.

Nickie shut off the pink beast and unstrapped. She popped up from the seat sporting a new florescent-blue hairdo and wearing jean cutoff shorts and a neon-pink tube top. As she stood there and shook her shoulders, she gave a big "Ta-da!"

Chasey and the Gypsy called out in unison as they stepped off the porch together, "Nickie!"

7

After the customary round of hugs when Nickie's feet hit the ground, the Gypsy asked, "How's everybody back home?"

Nickie replied with her loving smile, "Fine. Rachael sends her best and asked me to make sure you didn't need anything. And so does Jeb."

Chasey and the Gypsy looked at each other and smiled a gentle smile of comfort and understanding as he placed his arm around her shoulders and pulled her close. There was a lot of water under those bridges, and they had been burned.

"Tell her 'thank you' from both of us, Nickie," Chasey replied.

"Let me get your things," the Gypsy said. "We'll put you in the spare room. Chasey cleared the bed off quickly when we heard you coming. If she had bothered to tell me you were coming, I would have gotten the room cleaned up a little better." He shot her a curious, questioning look over his shoulder as he walked past Nickie.

"Sorry. It was a spur-of-the-moment thing. We got busy last night after I called and then I forgot," Chasey replied with a bat of her eyes, as she played dumb. She hoped he bought it.

"I know. The memory's the *second* thing to go when you get old."

Being a gullible sucker at times, Nickie asked, "What's the first?"

With a confused look on his face, he turned to look at her and replied after a brief pause, "I forgot."

Nickie gave him a little laugh and a smirk.

Chasey stomped her foot and yelled, "I'M NOT THE ONE WHO'S OLD, 'OLD' MAN!" Chasey placed her hands on her hips, arched her back, and stuck out her tongue at him to prove her point. Chasey's reaction to his little joke caused the Gypsy to smile from ear to ear.

A smile he kept until they got Nickie and her things settled into the spare room.

"You want to put a pan on to heat and go out and get some eggs while I help Nickie unpack, Blue-Eyes?" Chasey asked. She hoped to get a second alone with Nickie so she could explain what she witnessed and what her plan was to find out if he actually was up to anything.

"Sure. You two take your time and get caught up, and I'll get breakfast fixed."

"'Kay. Thanks," she was relieved. That gave them several minutes to talk. The Gypsy was a very slow cook. He was a good cook, just very slow at it.

After he went outside for the eggs, Chasey began to relay her suspicions as to the fact that the Gypsy was up to something. Just what he was up to, she had not a clue. She then laid out her plan to Nickie.

"I've got you a rental car. It's a Lexus with dark tinted windows. I have it parked next door out of sight so Blue-Eyes won't see it. The next time he takes out, you will be able to get in it and follow him down the road and easily catch up to him. He shouldn't get suspicious because we get a lot of visitors in the area who rent the same type of cars and drive the same way. Just stay behind him, and don't act like you want to pass, and everything will be fine."

Nickie nodded in agreement as the door opened and closed again.

"We've got three kids, babe!" the Gypsy called in as he put the eggs in the sink to wash. "I thought they weren't due for another couple of weeks?"

Chasey came running out with Nickie in tow. "Eh. They're a little early. We'll go check them out. How'd they look?" she asked as she grabbed her animal midwife bag she had in the mudroom.

"Fine. They were suckling away."

Chasey ducked out the back door followed by Nickie. "That was a bit of good luck as long as the *kids are all right*," Chasey said.

As soon as she finished the sentence, they both stopped dead in their tracks, looked at each other, and threw back their heads and laughed. After they finished their laugh, they grabbed hands and skipped like the little girlfriends they were into the pen where the goats were kept.

While the Gypsy stood at the kitchen sink and washed the eggs, he watched the strange scene unfold outside. He wondered if he just experienced a flashback from some of the drugs he took many years ago. But he knew both of them, and he was sure his eyes had *not* deceived him. Their actions caused him to smile. He shook his head in disbelief and went back to washing the eggs and preparing breakfast. He wondered, *What are those two doing?*

8

Five days passed since Nickie's arrival, and the Gypsy had not displayed any suspicious behavior that Nicki was able to notice. It drove Chasey crazy. Finally, toward the end of the week, they had some things that needed to be taken into town.

"We have some things that need to be taken to the recyclers today," Chasey started after she gave the new kids their morning checkup and gave them all a clean bill of health. "I'll ask if he would take the things into town and stop at the vets to let him know the kids came and are healthy week-olds. I'll tell him we're gonna stay here with them 'just in case.' Since they were a *little* early. Then you can slip off and follow him and see if he does anything suspicious."

"Sounds like a perfectly devious plan," Nickie replied with a perfectly devious smile as she tapped her fingers together and made her eyebrows walk across her forehead like worms on parade.

"Stop it, Nickie," Chasey chided. "Don't make it sound like *I'm* the one doing something wrong."

"You don't know *if* Blue-Eyes *is* doing anything at all… yet," Nickie replied curtly, with her hands on her hips, being sure to accent the important words in her response.

"You're right. But you didn't see the way he acted. I've *never* seen him act *that* way, okay?"

"Okay. We'll find out soon enough."

9

After the three of them ate the breakfast the Gypsy prepared, he washed the dishes, Nickie dried them, and Chasey put them away. After Chasey put the last of the dishes where they belonged, she turned to the Gypsy. As he hung the towel to dry that he took from Nickie, Chasey asked, "Would you mind going into town with the recyclables and stopping at the vet's? Nickie and I will stay here with the kids. Ask the vet to come out and give them a check since they were a little early. Be sure to let him know they're doing fine."

"Okay," he replied. He perked up a little like a dog that heard someone pull into the drive. "I... um... That will give you girls a chance to chitchat without me around," he added as he quickly moved over to where the keys were kept and picked them up. As he started toward the door, he threw his hand up as he always did and said, "'Kay. Bye."

Chasey and Nickie looked at one another with genuine concern, and Chasey quickly called out to him, "It's too early, you big dummy. Where are you going this early? The vet doesn't get in 'til noon."

The Gypsy knew he was caught. He thought quickly and, while he tried to look "like a big dummy," he said, "I didn't realize it was so early." He shuffled his feet to where they kept the keys and put them back. With his head hung down, he shuffled over to where Chasey stood with her hands on her hips. She stared at him as she shook her head slowly back and forth. The Gypsy kissed her on her forehead as he passed. He proceeded out back and continued with the tear-down and the sorting of the latest batch of salvaged materials.

"That was odd even for him, right?" Chasey asked quizzically of Nickie as soon as the Gypsy was outside and out of earshot.

"Yah. Even for him," Nickie responded. Unsure of what exactly Blue-Eyes was up to, she watched him shuffle all the way to the old machinery that was in various stages of being dismantled. "He's overselling it," she said as she looked back at Chasey.

"He's acting like a little kid," Chasey noticed.

"Ed Zachery! He knows he's been caught doing something. Like looking at his uncle's porn," Nickie said with a cross-eyed look and her tongue stuck out of the side of her mouth as she kicked at the floor with her left foot and gave a snap with her right hand.

"Nickie! GAWD. You and your descriptive imagery. When he leaves, you have to follow him," Chasey added with a slightly disgusted smirk as she slowly shook her head. She always did like Nickie's personality, even the weird parts.

"I'm on him like Chasey on a Recyclers' Convention," Nickie shot back with a shit-eatin' grin.

10

They got the trailer hooked up to the old Dodge, and then the Gypsy climbed in and headed off to town to deliver the load of recyclables. The Gypsy thought he would be able to check in with Kelly without Chasey being any the wiser.

After Nickie and Chasey waved goodbye to the Gypsy and watched him go out of sight, Nicki turned to face Chasey. She turned Chasey so her good ear faced her, and said, "Don't worry. I'm sure it's completely innocent. I'll not lose him."

They embraced, and Chasey handed her the keys to the car and said, "Then I don't need to tell you."

Nickie shook her head as she ran to where Chasey stashed her a rental car to use to "inconspicuously" follow Blue-Eyes. There she found a gleaming sliver Lexus LC500.

Granted, this thing would have no trouble keeping up with the old Dodge, but com' on, girl! This is the type of thing people rent around here? Nickie thought as she tore off down the road after the Gypsy. *I would have been just as well off to follow him in the rat rod.*

Nickie put the gas pedal of the Lexus to the floor to see what it had. It "had" plenty. The Lexus's acceleration caused Nickie to smile and forget momentarily what she was supposed to be doing. The rear end of the old Dodge, and the trailer full of recyclable material it pulled, came *very quickly* into view. When Nickie saw the back of the Gypsy's head in the old Dodge, it caused her to call the Lexus's brakes into operation. She hoped the breaks were as lust-worthy as the LC's acceleration. Luckily, they were, and she was able to bring the screaming rocket under control before she got close enough for the Gypsy to be able to recognize who was driving.

11

The Gypsy looked up into his rearview mirror in time to see "another damn tourist come flying up behind him just in a hurry to go nowhere fast." Chasey always laughed at him when he would complain about them that way. She would always follow the laugh with saying, "You're just waiting for the day when you can sit on your porch, shake your fist, and yell, 'You kids get out of my damn yard!' aren't you?"

That always made *him* laugh. At least this one was able to get stopped. "They're not driving a time machine." That was always his argument. "No matter how fast they drive, they're not going to make up for lost time." That was when she would pat him on his leg and say, "Yes, dear." Like that was supposed to make what *they* did all right. Oh well.

This bozo was not in too much of a hurry. They were not trying to pass or tailgate.

Hopefully that will keep 'til town, the Gypsy thought.

Nickie kept her distance until they reached the road before the scrap yard. Chasey told her she would be able to turn around and park there while she waited on the Gypsy until he finished with the recycling.

Nickie swept quickly left and drove a short distance down the very straight road before she slowly came to a stop. The road was lined with evergreen trees and the wood privacy fence of the scrap yard on one side. On the other side, there was the large dogleg of a stream and a wooded area. After she stopped, she checked to make sure the road was clear. She threw the car into reverse for a "moonshiner's turn" to get the car turned around and headed in the opposite direction while she waited for the Gypsy to leave the scrap yard.

While she sat there and waited for the Gypsy, she thought she would call Chasey and mess with her. That's assuming she even answered the phone.

The phone rang. Three, four, five times, and then the machine picked up with Chasey's message, "You know the drill," and then *beep*!

OH MY GOD! Nickie thought. *How can she always give me grief for being so nostalgic when she won't even get a cell phone but she uses the same answering machine message as that lame '90's show* 90210 *wannabe heartthrob did.*

Nickie spoke into the phone, "Thelma calling Louise. Come in, Louise. *All quiet on the western front.*" And then she hung up.

The Gypsy pulled up to the exit of the scrap yard with an empty trailer about half an hour after he entered. He pulled out onto the road and headed back in the direction he came. That was the direction Nickie took a chance he would go. Luckily, Chasey told her that it shouldn't take longer than half an hour at the scrap yard even if someone talked to him because of their strict no-loitering policy.

"Mr. Mullan runs a tight ship," Chasey told her.

So she figured, if after thirty or so minutes she did not see him pass, she could take off down the road. With her in the Lexus and the Gypsy in the Dodge, she probably stood a fair chance of catching him.

But that was all moot now because here he came, right on time. She let him go down the road ahead of her for a ten-count before she started up and followed him. More slowly this time. She did not need to run him over, and she already knew what this car could do.

As they entered the main section of town, Nickie drifted closer to the Gypsy as she tried to anticipate where he might go. By his head gestures and then slowing, he indicated he was likely beginning a left turn into the blacksmith's parking lot. Nickie made a quick right onto the side street at the corner florists. She parked and went into *Bauer's Flowers*. Nickie positioned herself in front of the big bay window that faced the street opposite the blacksmith's so she could see the odd block or so down to the forge where the Gypsy did "whatever."

As Nickie stood there and tried to imagine just what kind of "trouble" Blue-Eyes got into at the forge, she felt the presence of the florist, Rosemond Bauer, approach her from behind.

When Rosemond got to Nickie's shoulder, she inquired in a thick, proper German accent with more than just a little bit of haughtiness, "May I help..." Rosemond paused as she looked Nickie up and down. She arched an eyebrow and looked quite like some snobbish butler about to turn away a couple of street urchins. "Madam? Find anything today?" she finally asked in that questioning tone that always got Nickie's motor going. But lucky for her, today she was on a mission and did not have time for her bigotry.

So Nickie bit the inside of her cheek and replied, "I'm here checking up on my best friend's old man. It's Chasey MacDonald, if you know her. She thinks her old man might be up to something. She said he's been acting strange. He just went into the blacksmith's."

"And just what does Chasey think ole Blue-Eyes is up to?"

Nickie relaxed a little. Hearing this woman call him Blue-Eyes meant she must at least know *of* them. "She's afraid he might be getting back to his old ways."

"Well, *die Arbeiterin*, I can tell you with complete confidence that he is not being unfaithful with anyone over there."

Nickie turned around for the first time since she arrived in the flower shop to face Rosemond. She was a large German woman of "fine stock" who looked like she lived up to her surname well. She was dressed to the nines in a flowered dress with rain boots and a large, brown apron. "And just how do you know?" Nickie asked as she placed her hands on her hips to mirror Rosemond's statuesque image that stood before her.

"Two reasons—one, because Magnus is as faithful as the day is long to that wife of his, he's not gay, and he's a little bit scared of the Gypsy." They both smiled a little at that. "And two, *he's* not Kelly's type."

"How do you know that? He used to be a pro."

"Because she's my daughter, *she's* gay, and I know the real reason why he's there. Sort of."

"Oh, do tell!" Nickie asked with added haughty enthusiasm.

"Well, I don't go tellin' tales to just anybody who walks into *my* store. Just who are you, *das kind*?" Rosemond demanded sternly.

"I'm Nickie Pantani. I'm Chasey's best friend. That's who I am!"

Rosemond chuckled, "So you're *Nikola*, hum. The feisty little Italian spark plug of whom little *Fräulein* MacDonald speaks of so fondly, huh?"

Nickie shot her a smug, disapproving look.

"All I know is this. Kelly came home saying 'It's about time!' and extremely excited. But she said she couldn't tell me anything about it. Just that Blue-Eyes asked her to make something for him. I'm sure Chasey has no reason to worry."

Nickie could tell she told the truth. Or at least what she thought was the truth. After she bid farewell to Frau Bauer, she decided to head back to Chasey's house and report back to her on what she found. She needed to be sure that she left out the part that she might get a *damn engagement ring!*

Before she got back on the road to Chasey's, Nickie thought she would have a little more fun with her. So she called her one more time and hoped she would not answer. Three rings, four rings, five rings, "You know the drill," and then *beep!*

Nickie said, "Huck calling Tom. Come in, Tom. We're on *The Road Back*." Nickie hung up and headed back toward Chasey's. She felt a little full of herself.

12

The Gypsy stopped in front of the blacksmith's. He had a little feeling of déjà vu. He was sure that was the same car that almost ran over him earlier. They turned off anyway. He had more important things on his mind than to worry about what some crazy tourist was in a hurry to see.

He parked the truck and trailer on the street so as to be able to easily leave and not have to worry about trying to back out. He was able to do it. He just hated having to do it more than getting skunked. So he avoided it at every opportunity.

The Gypsy walked into the forge. After he and Magnus exchanged their usual greetings of nods and waves, he proceeded back to where Kelly worked on some project for another customer. Kelly saw the Gypsy as he approached. She stopped grinding on the sword that she worked on and smiled at him.

"Looks like a nice piece," the Gypsy queried since he wanted to know more about it.

"It's for an out-of-state customer. They saw my work on the internet and asked for a custom piece," Kelly responded as she held the curvy dagger blade up for him to admire. "The blade itself won't be too fancy, but the engravings and etchings on everything should be. I just have to keep the customer from going overboard. I'm going to send them pictures in what 'I deem' finished stages so that hopefully they won't overembellish it."

The Gypsy nodded his understanding and approval.

"I've got you some design drawings ready. I think you'll be happy. Might even get a smile out of you."

"Don't hold your breath," he responded in an ever-so-slightly harsh tone but with that crooked grin of his.

Kelly responded by crinkling her nose back at him as she produced her sketchbook with the renderings of her ideas for Chasey's ring. She lay it flat on the work bench for the Gypsy to view two pages at once. In the center of each page were two large images of differing designs. The large images were surrounded by smaller sketches. They were of design ideas that Kelly had for Chasey's ring in various stages of completion. The two in the center of the pages were the ones Kelly wanted to sell. They were the ones on which she spent the most time.

The first ring looked a lot like his ring from the military, just slimmed down, and instead of the black onyx as the center stone, a diamond solitaire was displayed. The solitaire was surrounded by the rubies and diamond chips. She encrusted the sides of the ring with the onyx.

While nice, the Gypsy thought it looked more like something a man would wear. The one on the other page was a two-piece design of engagement ring and wedding band that went together. They were definitely more feminine-looking than the first.

Kelly watched the Gypsy's face, as she watched all her clients' faces, so she would know when to step in with comments. She saw a sparkle in his eye when he looked at the main image on the second page. It was her favorite as well.

"I made that in two separate parts. After you get married, if Chasey wants, I can fuse them together at the bottom," she said while she pointed to the area where she would be able to connect the two pieces. "The only thing I didn't use were the rubies. I didn't think they would work."

The Gypsy stood there and nodded as he looked at the image. He tried to imagine what it would look like. The solitaire sat higher than they usually did on engagement rings of this size. The solitaire was not much more than a half carat, he guessed, from his limited knowledge of such things. It was surrounded by four stones cut from the onyx. The way the stones were mounted, it looked like the sides of a cauldron. It looked like the solitaire sat above the rim of the cauldron. She placed a diamond chip on each side of the mountain of stones. They bridged the gap in the ring. Where the cauldron came over empty space was where the wedding band was designed to fit. It was roughly shaped like a heart with a diamond chip on each side at the beginning of the bend that lined up with the chips on the other ring.

The Gypsy noticed how much the wedding band resembled a heart. He asked Kelly, "Could you put the rubies on the heart-shaped part of the band? Or are they too big?"

"You know, I never even thought of that," Kelly said in amazement. She pulled out her colored pencils and quickly added the details. The change would definitely be worth it.

"I think we have a winner," the Gypsy said with confidence and ever so slight a smile.

"Hah! I almost got one," Kelly said with a point that she followed with a clap of her hands as she rocked back on her stool.

"How long do you think it will take you to finish it?"

"I already have everything I need to make it. If you're positive on this design?"

"You know her tastes as well as I do. She likes your work. That's why I came to you to make it."

"I know. Thanks. It shouldn't take me longer than three weeks, but in case I get busy here... let's say a month."

"Okay. No rush. You know I'd rather it be right than early. I'll stop by in a month then," he said as he pushed away from the bench and then headed out with a wave.

The Gypsy hated to rush, but he did not want to be away too long and have to try to lie to Chasey if she asked what kept him.

13

After Nickie parked the Lexus back in its hiding place, she skipped back to Chasey's like a little schoolgirl who returned from recess with the latest gossip. She went around to the back of the house to where Chasey took apart some particularly nasty-looking piece of machinery. Nickie stopped beside Chasey. With her hands behind her back, she stood there and grinned from ear to ear while she swung her arms back and forth.

Nickie was barely able to contain herself but was able to manage, "You have *nothing* to worry about. I can't tell you anything more right now, but I will stay for a little while to help you if you want me to."

Chasey jumped up from where she squatted and turned a wrench. "WHAT THE HELL IS HE UP TO, NICKIE?" she screamed. She grabbed Nickie by the shoulders and, as she shook her vigorously, inquired, "Has he started using heroin again?"

"No!" Nickie said in a very firm tone as she threw Chasey's hands off her shoulders in a show of disgust because she suggested he fell off the wagon. "Come on. You know he's stronger than that."

"Then he's gone back to work turning tricks, or... or..." Chasey could not bring herself to say that he cheated on her.

"He is not being unfaithful to you."

"You know how good he was. Word gets around. He made *really* good money. Or maybe he's just tired of me," she added dejectedly.

"Chasey, Blue-Eyes loves you. You're both asexual. Yes, he's *amazing*—in bed and out of bed. And in the field and the pool. And pretty much anywhere and everywhere," Nickie explained as she placed her hands on Chasey's shoulders to comfort her. "But trust me, *he* is not doing *anything* you need to worry about. Okay? You'll find out soon enough." Nickie pulled Chasey in and hugged her. She added with a grin, "You're gonna like it. I promise."

"Okay," Chasey responded as she shook her head. "I'll trust you. But... wha—" she stammered as she tried to say more.

Nickie gently shook her and said, "You have to just force yourself to not think about it. All right? Put it out of your mind. I saw what he was doing. It's fine! So *chill*."

Chasey relaxed a little, exhaled a deep breath and said, "All right, I will."

Nickie helped Chasey tear down the old harvester she worked on while they waited for the Gypsy to return. About half an hour later, he showed up with an empty truck and trailer and a well-placed "dumb look" on his face.

14

As Nickie, Chasey, and the Gypsy sat at the kitchen table and finished their breakfast, the Gypsy tried to come up with an excuse to go see Kelly about the ring. A month passed since he saw her renderings of the ring and gave the go-ahead. If he was ever this excited before, he did not remember. He tried to come up with something to use for an excuse to go to town but kept coming up blank. He thought about breaking something. But he did not want to repair something if it did not *have* to be repaired.

They were out doing some morning chores when good fortune smiled upon him. Chasey broke the handle on her hoe. She came around the shed with a playful pout on her face to where the Gypsy adjusted the carburetor on an old rototiller that they salvaged and were reconditioning. She walked up to him and said in a little girl voice, "Fix it, Blue-Eyes."

He just shook his head and asked, "What is wrong with you? Test this tiller out, and I'll go get you a new one. Do we need anything else while I'm going?"

"A 6mm socket. I broke one yesterday," she replied as she spoke in her normal voice and gave her attention to the rototiller.

"Let's not make this a habit," he said with a chuckle. He called out to where Nickie fed some baby chicks, "You need anything, Nickie?"

"No, I'm good" was her only reply.

The Gypsy checked the shopping list after he grabbed the truck keys and headed out the door, happy that he was able to go to town unfettered and check in on Kelly and her progress on the ring.

15

The Gypsy left out of the drive and went as fast as the old Dodge was capable.

"But not too fast," he told himself. "Keep your cool. You don't want to tip her off." He kept going over in his head what he needed to get. "Hoe handle, 6mm socket. Hoe handle, 6mm socket. Hoe handle, 6mm socket." If he forgot one of them, the only thing that would grant him forgiveness would be the ring. "Hoe handle, 6mm socket. Hoe handle, 6mm socket. Hoe handle, 6mm socket."

As he pulled through town, he slowed while he passed the blacksmith's shop. Magnus and Kelly were propped up out front as they enjoyed the morning air. As the Gypsy slowed, he threw up his index finger at them to indicate "give me just a minute". His action caused Kelly and Magnus to exchange confused looks as he passed. He continued on down the road and around the corner to where the hardware store was and purchased the hoe handle and 6mm socket and then headed back to the blacksmith's.

When the Gypsy arrived back at the blacksmith's, Magnus and Kelly were still leaning against the fence in front of the forges. As he approached, he explained the little detour.

When he finished, Kelly asked, "I guess you're here to see the ring. Well, it's finished. Wanna see it?"

The Gypsy looked over at Magnus, and Magnus threw up his basketball-sized shoulders and catcher's mitt hands as if to say, "I don't know."

The Gypsy looked back at Kelly and said sarcastically, "No, I just wanted to see if I could get you to make it."

"Smart-ass. Come on. I'm not sure if Chasey deserves this ring from *you*, at least," she said as she waved him in behind her.

Kelly and the Gypsy left Magnus to his musings and went inside to where she had the finished projects and precious items locked safely inside a walk-in safe "cleverly" disguised as a wall-mounted water cooler. She retrieved the ring and took it and the Gypsy into the showing room where they both sat down in very comfortable cognac leather–upholstered, wingback chairs. The chairs had very tall, narrow backs that were extremely vertical. They also had shorter seating areas and lower arms than normal. The short seat area and upright back made them the perfect chairs in which to sit to view objects under a magnifying glass and bright light.

As Kelly sat down, she looked into the Gypsy's eyes, and he looked back into hers. She knew he would not be impressed with the ring's artistic beauty, just the quality of the work that went into making it. And she said so with a smirk on her face, "I know you won't be impressed with the whole design and how 'pretty' it is." As she wrinkled her nose at him, she used air quotes to emphasize *pretty*. She continued, "So I'll just tell you, Chasey's going to love that part of it. And I'll ask you the only part you're interested in, 'Is the work up to *your* standards?'"

"Eh, I've seen better," he responded in his best smart-ass voice followed with that ever-so-slight smile as he looked up from the ring. Of course, he had not seen much to equal. Kelly was one of the best. She could easily have worked for Cartier back in the day even though her style was a little different. "I'm sure she will love it. Putting the rubies on the wedding band really worked."

"I thought so too. I left them off at first to see what the rings would look like. The band alone didn't work without the rubies. But when you add the rubies, the band can stand alone. So if Chasey decides she doesn't want to fuse the two together like I had suggested, she could just wear the band and it would not look plain."

The Gypsy separated both rings. He placed the engagement ring on his right hand and left the band on his left. That way, they could look at the difference between when it was with the engagement ring and not. They both nodded in agreement as to how well it looked. The four tiny ruby chips on the heart-ish shaped dip in the band were flanked by a diamond chip.

"That'll do. How much?"

"Since I didn't use all of the onyx or gold, how's fifteen sound?"

"Thousand! Are you high?" the Gypsy exclaimed with a face of sheer horror. He knew what she really meant.

Kelly looked at him with her hands placed firmly on her broad hips. If she wore glasses, she would have looked over her glasses at him.

"Oh, dollars. Cool."

"Don't make me get Magnus in here, old man," Kelly scolded.

The Gypsy 'tee-heed' as he pulled out his billfold to pay her. "Fifteen hundred will be just fine, dear. I'm sure Chasey will love it."

16

Kelly told the Gypsy if the size was off or if there was *anything* Chasey did not like about the ring to be sure and bring it back *immediately*. They hugged, and he thanked her yet again. He made his way out of the blacksmith's shop and bid his usual farewell to Magnus, who looked to have not moved an inch since his arrival. The Gypsy climbed back into the old Dodge with the ring box tucked firmly in his shirt pocket and headed down the road back toward home.

As he drove back home, he tried to come up with a clever way to give Chasey her ring. But he was never good at clever. He thought about all those romance movies she made him watch and what some of the people did in them. But the good ideas had already been done to death.

He strained his brain as he tried to come up with a neat way to propose. A proposal that would make her blush and Nickie go crazy. One that would be worthy of those stupid movies they made him watch.

"What is it with women and that crap?" he asked himself. "Why can't you just say 'HERE!' and be done with it?"

As he mused to himself, a blaring truck horn and flashing lights brought the Gypsy back to focus. He brought the Dodge back into his lane and avoided a head-on collision with the mail truck.

"Whoa! Old man, pay attention," he scolded himself. "What's wrong with you? You have to get home in one piece."

After he composed himself, he thought, *Wouldn't that be some shit? Get my dumb ass killed in a fiery crash on the way home and all they find in the ashes is the ring?*

He shook his head and thought, *What a morbid thought. What's wrong with me?* He pulled over at the first place he could. *Is this just cold feet? It had to be. I love her, and she me, and she wants to spend the rest of her life with me. And I want to do the same. Period.*

The Gypsy put the Dodge back in gear and headed home. He still did not know how he would give the ring to Chasey. As he pulled into the drive, Nickie and Chasey were in the side lot with some recyclables. They stacked them in the trailer as he turned off the truck.

He got out of the truck, and Chasey asked, "Did you remember the socket?"

The Gypsy tossed Chasey the bag that contained the socket. When he got close enough, he used the hoe handle to help him get down on one knee in front of her. He tossed it high so she would have to reach above her head and would not be looking directly at him. After he tossed the bag with the socket, he retrieved the ring box from his pocket as he went down on one knee. He released the hoe handle, and as it hit the ground, he used that hand to open the ring box, and asked, "Chasey, will you marry me?"

17

When Nickie would tell this story later, she would swear she heard Chasey crap her pants, but it was doubtful anything was heard over Nickie's squealing. That was the only thing that could be heard for over a mile for about twenty minutes. Chasey was glad to be deaf in her left ear for the first time since the wreck, and the Gypsy swore he lost a good deal of the hearing in his right ear from all the squealing. Chasey did not think her heart took a beat or that she was even able to breath for a good half an hour after the proposal.

Chasey dropped down to her knees in front of the Gypsy. She looked at the rings. Her hands shook as she reached toward them and said, "It's beautiful."

The Gypsy took the rings out because Chasey had trouble doing it. Her hands shook as he placed them on the ring finger of her left hand and then kissed them.

After he did, he looked back into her eyes and said, "I love you, Chasey. I'm sorry this took so long."

Chasey fell into him. She was fully involved in tears and an emotional wreck. Her life was finally fulfilled. After all the hell they went through, they finally got to settle down and get married. She had never been happier.

Chasey finally managed to get herself under control, a little. Enough at least to push back out of his arms and look him in the eyes and say, "I love you too, Blue-Eyes. And I want to spend the rest of my life with you. Yes, I will marry you."

After Chasey finished her confirmation to the Gypsy's proposal, Nickie ran in and dove on the two of them and squealed, "I am soooo happy for the two of you!"

"What took you so long?" Chasey asked after she thumped him on his chest. "I was having the worst thoughts about what you were up to."

The Gypsy shrugged and looked back at her like a little boy who just handed his grade-school sweetheart the ring he got from his "Cracker Jack's."

"That's why Nickie's here," she exclaimed as she slapped her on the back of her shoulder. "I called her! To spy on you!"

The Gypsy looked over at Nickie and asked, "Was that you the other day that almost rear-ended me in the gray import?"

"Yes," Nickie replied. Feeling a little embarrassed, she grabbed his arm and hid her face on it. "I let it get away from me. THAT THING IS A BEAST!"

"Now, don't go and blame the car for your hot-rodin' little lady," the Gypsy said with a sarcastic scolding tone.

His comment got him the tongue and the single-finger salute.

With a smile, the Gypsy exclaimed, "I guess this calls for a celebration. What's say let's go into town and get something to eat and a bottle of champagne?"

"Definitely," agreed Chasey.

"Yes. I'll go ahead and pack up and head out after we eat so I can get back and give everyone the news," Nickie added. "I've been here long enough keeping an 'eye' on nothing," she said as she looked through her thumb and index finger of her right hand at the Gypsy.

The Gypsy shot a steely look back at Nickie and then proceeded to stick his tongue out at her.

"You don't *have* to run back, but I know you have things to do back home," Chasey said. "Why don't you go ahead and get cleaned up first. Then I'll clean up while you and Blue-Eyes pack your stuff." She turned to the Gypsy and asked, "You won't need a shower, will you? You haven't done anything that you can't just rag off?"

He responded in an annoyed but joking tone, "I could have worn what I have on if *someone* hadn't tackled me in the yard!"

Chasey smiled, leaned in, kissed him, and said, "You deserved to be tackled." She patted him on his chest as she got up and offered her hand to him to help him up. They both groaned from the effort and had a little chuckle.

18

After they loaded everything Nickie brought with her into the Jeep, Chasey and the Gypsy climbed into the old Dodge and headed down the road toward Chasey's favorite restaurant. La Pelle Rouillée. Oddly, it was not a classical French restaurant. But it was a *good* restaurant. The restaurant had your basic fare of steaks, chicken, and local wild game. It also had stuff you expected to see in Paris with names no one could pronounce and descriptions of dishes no one wanted to try. The customers always tried them at least once and still wondered a year later if they liked it or not.

As they drove through the center of town, Chasey and the Gypsy looked at each other and shook their heads at the roar of Nickie's rat rod. The old Dodge was not quiet by any stretch of the imagination. Sound dampening was not used much in work trucks from the thirties. Even so, it was not a loud ride. Nickie's Jeep could be heard clearly behind them.

"Next time she comes, she needs to have mufflers on that thing," the Gypsy said. He noticed he spoke a little louder than normal. It was not just because it was Chasey's bad side but also because Nickie's rat rod was just that damn loud.

"I know. It was an emergency. She doesn't usually drive it like that, but her other car was down," Chasey replied loudly.

As they made their approach to the restaurant, you were able to see why they called it The Rusty Shovel. Outside—leaning, hanging, or somehow arranged—were every implement of destruction known to man. There were wheelbarrows far past their usefulness for toting that were used as herb gardens. Various trowels and spades were turned into wind chimes. To some, this place was heaven. Others... a nightmare.

The restaurant was in an old ranch house that had a dilapidated picket fence around the house that had lost almost all of its whitewash. There was a large arbor with a very old wisteria that grew over it to the point that it became difficult to tell where the arbor ended and the wisteria began. Someone took great care of it over the years. They trained the vine and pruned it to keep it in shape.

When you got inside, it reminded you of any number of chain restaurants with "meh" menus. The only difference, here the food was amazing. It looked like they raided every yard sale, thrift store, and dollar store within one hundred miles to decorate the place. Chasey liked to look at all the junk when they were there. The Gypsy liked to watch her reaction when she discovered a new piece of junk. And they both *loved* the food. The wait staff were friendly and not overly aggressive or pretensive.

After they finished their celebration, Nickie jumped back in her rat rod and got all buckled in. Before firing it up, she said, "I'll be sure and let everybody back home know the good news."

"Thanks, Nickie. Have a safe trip home," Chasey replied after she leaned down and gave Nickie a hug goodbye.

Chasey stepped back next to the Gypsy. After she stepped back, Nickie started the Jeep. As she did, the Gypsy waved and said loudly, "Be careful."

Nickie backed out of her parking place, put the Jeep in drive and threw up her hand. Then with a loud roar of exhaust, a grumble of tires on pavement, and Nickie's squeal of excitement, she tore down the road and headed back home. While Chasey and the Gypsy stood there and looked at each other, they shook their heads and smiled at the sight and sound of Nickie as she left.

"That girl," the Gypsy said as he opened the door to the Dodge for Chasey to get in the truck. After they got in, he drove them back to what would be "their" home for hopefully a very long time.

19

Chasey and the Gypsy arrived back at their homestead before the sun started to set. They put the things away that had places and left things in the kitchen that would not go bad. They went into the bath and shared a shower together. After they dressed, they both got glasses to drink. Water without ice and a slice of lime for the Gypsy and some green tea and honey for Chasey.

They went outside and gave the farm animals the attention they needed and proceeded to their favorite spot to relax... the hammock swing. The two of them made it from leftover lumber for the framework and some metalwork Magnus made for them to "pretty it up," as he said. Chasey and the Gypsy made the macramé seat themselves with salvaged rope from a store sell-off or delivery mishap of some kind. The Gypsy was never sure just where she found all the salvage opportunities, but she was like a pig on a truffle when it came to finding salvage opportunities.

The Gypsy sat down first and then Chasey beside him, as usual. They sat there and watched the sunset. Chasey noticed something she never saw before. He was smiling. Not that he never smiled before. If he found something amusing or funny, he smiled, but this was different.

"What's so funny?" Chasey asked.

He looked at her a little confused and responded, "What do you mean?"

"You're smiling. I've never seen you smile before unless you found something funny."

He thought about that for a second and then answered, "I guess I'm just happy."

"You weren't happy before?"

He thought for a moment and then responded, "I've never been married before."

Chasey climbed across the Gypsy and kissed him like he had never been kissed before. She stopped kissing him, leaned back and looked into his eyes the color of the Caribbean Sea with flecks of slate and teal and said with a smirk upon her lips, "But you're not married, yet."

"Wait… what?"

Part IV

Wild Cat

1

The Gypsy and Chasey sat on the porch of their cabin and enjoyed the breeze. Several years passed since the Gypsy proposed to Chasey. She finally got him to agree to a date and go ahead with the wedding. He always came up with some excuse as to why they could not get married. The only reason he agreed to the date she set was because Chasey threatened to beat the Gypsy to within an inch of his life. When he was in a talkative mood, she would have to find out what his aversion to actually getting married was.

They enjoyed their lemonades while they sat on the porch and rested after they did their morning chores. As they sat there, they heard the unmistakable thundering roar of a Harley as it came down their dirt path. Sure enough, a short time later, a Fat Boy lumbered into view. But this was not a beer-bellied biker you expected to find riding such a demon. This wild cat had legs that looked a little too familiar to the Gypsy. But they were attached to what appeared to be not much more than a child. Sixteen at best—with flaming red hair just a little darker than strawberry-blond but not as dark as auburn.

When she stopped at the end of the path to the cabin and put the kick stand down, Chasey got a good look at her. She realized who she was and went inside. She knew about this child before she left to find the Gypsy all those long years ago but never told him about her. Something always seemed to either take precedent or prevented her from remembering that she needed to tell him.

As the wild cat swung one of her long legs over the bike to get off, the Gypsy took a look at the boots she wore. He saw them somewhere before; he was sure of it. They were quite impressive. Ostrich skin with a lot of embellishments. As she walked toward him in what was almost a two-step of a gait, he noticed the cowgirl hat that was all she had on her head as she rode up.

Something familiar about that hat too, he thought. *This is not going to end well for me.*

The Gypsy then took in what little there was of clothing. A faintly pink spaghetti-string tank top with no bra. He was fairly sure the child probably never wore one either. And she had the kind of breasts that caused wars. The cut-off jean shorts she wore were cut off so short and split so far up the side she may as well have not worn anything at all. She basically looked like every dirty old man's wet dream.

As the wild cat approached him, she smiled. If his legs had the strength to pick him up, he would run from there and never stop. Was that…?

The Gypsy thought he might have even wet himself as the wild cat got to the cabin and threw one long leg up on the porch as she looked down at the Gypsy over a pair of dark sunglasses with blue eyes that the Gypsy saw every time he looked in the mirror and asked, "Are you the one they call Gypsy?"

Well, fuck me! the Gypsy thought as he nodded slowly in confirmation. That was all he was able to bring himself to do. The wild cat reached into the messenger sack she carried, pulled out a letter and handed it to him.

2

Chasey had heard of this child and knew who she was. She was fairly sure she knew who her parents were, and her eyes were cut sharply at the father right now. Chasey heard rumors of an auburn-haired girl, born to one of the local "rich bitches" who frequently used the Gypsy's services. She was born with eyes the color of the Caribbean Sea with flecks of slate and teal that were ever so slightly cocked in the head as to always look just a little sad.

She was not sure she ever met her mother, but she knew her name. She was supposed to have been the third wife of an oil magnate who was very grateful for his prenup after he caught her for the third time in the one year of their short marriage in a compromising position with someone other than Mr. Oil Magnate. But Chasey was sure she was about to find out everything now. And just in time for their wedding too.

Chasey took a deep breath and stepped back out onto the porch. She brought a pitcher of lemonade and another glass that she filled as she joined the Gypsy and the redheaded stranger. She offered the glass to the wild cat and then topped off her and the Gypsy's glasses as he opened the letter and read it.

> Gypsy,
>
> By now you've looked into your own eyes and realized who she is and who is writing to you. The times we spent together were the best of my life. I was so happy and sad when Chasey and you left to start your life together. I didn't tell Chasey about your daughter after her accident

for obvious reasons. Forgive me if you disagree with them.

Shortly after our daughter was born, I started having health problems.

The Gypsy looked up at his daughter momentarily. He found her staring intently at him. He returned to his letter and continued reading.

I never fully regained my strength and developed an infection that in my weakened health did a number on my internal organs. After I regained what I was going to of my health, I fought various health issues until I was diagnosed with uterine cancer. No need to dwell on what happened.

I hope you and Chasey will show her the same love the two of you show everyone. To have never met you, she has so much of you in her. I hope she doesn't have my wild heart. Please keep her safe and raise her well.

All my best,
Chasity Monroe

After the Gypsy finished the letter, he summoned what little strength he had and stood. He took a step to where his daughter leaned against the porch post, took her into his arms and held her tightly. She wrapped her arms around her father for the first time and began to cry.

No one said anything for some time. Chasey walked up and joined them in a group embrace because she could not think of anything else to say or do. After Chasey put her arms around the Gypsy and his daughter, the Gypsy put one of his arms around her, looked down at her, and smiled.

After a couple of deep breaths, he finally spoke, "I guess we should gather your things and get them into *your* room, huh?"

He guided the two women in his life toward the Harley that sat in front of their home. He looked down at his daughter and asked, "So what do I call my little wild cat anyway?"

"Charity. Charity Monroe-Smith. Mom thought I should have your name too."

"Wait a minute," Chasey said as she came to an abrupt halt. "What *is* your name? I've always just called you Blue-Eyes. Since we're getting married, SOON"—she added in exclamation—"I should probably know."

The Gypsy was a little bashful about his name. He hem-hawed around for a second. He eventually said, "It's Smith. John Smith."

"JOHN SMITH!" Chasey exclaimed. She looked stunned and did not actually believe him.

"Yep. Just plain old John Smith."

"You're kidding, old man?"

The Gypsy reached back, pulled out his billfold, and as he removed his license to show her, he continued, "No, really. Just plain old John Smith. Nothing exciting or exotic. That's why I always liked Gypsy and Blue-Eyes. That's what most people call me everywhere I go anyway," he finished with a shrug.

"So I'm gonna be 'Mrs. Smith'?"

"I guess it could be worse. You could be Mrs. Robinson—although that's just kinda bad for me, ain't it?"

They both giggled and rubbed noses.

Charity looked at them both, as teenagers do, confused, and then finally before she felt the urge to barf, said, "I don't get it."

Her father turned to her and said, "Good! Now, let's get your things into your room," he finished with a chuckle.

"Mom warned me you were a little weird."

"A little weird?" Chasey exclaimed as she jerked her thumb at the Gypsy. "Charity, dear, Little Weird is his baby brother."

The Gypsy stopped dead in his tracks. His abrupt stop caused Chasey to run into his back.

"Oh!" Chasey exclaimed as she ran into his back and let out a grunt. "Very funny. But you know it's true," she added as she patted him on the back while they stood there.

The Gypsy had not moved or spoken since he stopped. Chasey and Charity walked past him and looked at him.

Chasey asked him with a genuine look of concern, "What's the matter, Blue-Eyes?"

The Gypsy just came to the realization that the women with whom he was the closest, with the exception of Nickie, had names that started with the same letters. They even sounded similar.

"Daddy?"

When he heard his daughter call him Daddy, it snapped him from his thoughts. He spoke, as he looked toward the both of them, "And I don't even want to get into it about all your names."

He continued on to the Harley to retrieve his daughter's things. Chasey and Charity stood there and looked at each other with looks of utter disbelief at what came out of his mouth.

Chasey motioned with both hands toward the Gypsy and said, "I present exhibit A."

3

The three of them retrieved all of Charity's things and placed them in the house in one trip. It was a good thing, too, because just as they got everything inside, a summer shower opened up. Charity and her father rushed out, grabbed the bike and pushed it onto the porch. Luckily, the wide tires of the Fat Boy made it easy to push up the two steps onto the porch and out of the rain.

"Thanks, Daddy."

"You're welcome..." the Gypsy paused and swallowed as he looked at her when she called him Daddy. Shortly, he added, "sweetheart."

Charity hugged him. As they went inside he added, "I'll get us a couple of towels to dry off with."

The Gypsy tossed Charity a towel to dry off with and dried himself with the other one he brought. Chasey stood there and watched them dry off. She thought about how much the two of them looked alike as they stood there together.

While she stood there and held a bag of Charity's things, she could not resist the opportunity to give the Gypsy a hard time and said, "Y'all just gonna stand there? Or does anybody wanna give me a hand with this?"

The Gypsy recognized her sarcastic tone. He quickly responded without even looking at her, "You look like you got it. We're fine."

Chasey shot him a look he was able to feel.

"Daddy?" Charity asked, unsure just how to respond.

"It's all right, dear. We're just playing," Chasey interjected quickly. "He knows my tones without looking."

The Gypsy looked at his daughter and grinned from ear to ear while Chasey explained.

"Oh," Charity replied with a little laugh. "I have to remember, Mom said you were weird."

"As advertised," the Gypsy said as he playfully tossed his towel into Charity's face. After he did, he took both towels back and put them in the laundry. Charity and her father finished gathering the rest of her things and found them a place in the guest room which was to become *her* room.

"Tomorrow we'll get what you won't need out of here and get you a desk for school," commented Chasey after Charity entered the room behind her father.

"What grade will you be going into this fall?" the Gypsy asked.

"Junior. One more after that and I'm done," Charity said as she made a swiping motion with one hand.

"Wrong!" Chasey and the Gypsy replied in unison. Their reply generated a strange look of confusion from Charity.

The Gypsy motioned toward Chasey to continue as he backed away. *Why not let her play the heavy?* The Gypsy thought. *That way I get to keep my daughter's love and get to be the fun one. Plus, Chasey is better at explaining things than I am. Win-win for me.*

Chasey took a deep calming breath and thought where best to begin. "Just because your father and I are not much more than glorified garbagemen, we are *fairly* educated," she said as she raised an eyebrow when she looked at the Gypsy.

With an insulted look, the Gypsy placed his hands on his hips and gave "Wait, what?" as his response.

Chasey and Charity laughed at the Gypsy, and then Charity asked, "Why?"

The Gypsy motioned to Chasey to finish what she started, so she continued, "Even if you do not start off college pursuing your declared degree, you need to start somewhere. And *never* stop learning. You don't have to stay in school, but you should always try to learn something new every day."

The Gypsy stood there with his arms crossed and nodded in agreement. Chasey looked over at him and added, "Before it becomes too late. You know the old saying, 'You can't teach an old dog new tricks.'" She looked back at Charity as she jerked her thumb in the Gypsy's direction.

"Now, wait a minute. How did this turn into 'pick on the old man'?"

Charity looked down and replied, "Oh. I was looking forward to being over it. I was over it years ago."

"Really? I loved school," Chasey said with enthusiasm.

"Well, you're definitely my kid. I hated school too. That's why I went into the service. There was no way in hell I was going to go to college after high school."

"Do you regret not going, Dad?"

The Gypsy stepped back for a moment and looked away. As he faced away from his girls, he eventually responded, "I don't *regret* it, but I kinda would have liked to have done *something*. Maybe a vocational school after I got out of the service. I couldn't see myself in a traditional school." He looked back over his shoulder and added, "Still can't."

4

After Chasey, Charity and the Gypsy finished supper, they cleaned the kitchen. When they finished in the kitchen, they went out and checked on their animals. While they were outside with the animals, Chasey took the time to introduce Charity to Gracie and the others. When the introductions were complete, they went inside and got ready for bed. It was a little early, but after the emotional day everyone had, an early bed time was what they all needed. After the Gypsy made sure the house was locked, everyone went to bed. It was a long, stressful day, and the Gypsy was ready for it to be over. He lay there on his back with Chasey lying next to him with an arm and leg thrown over him. He wasn't sure if she was asleep yet or not, but he was not able to sleep, and it would not come soon for him. As he lay there, he thought about the events of the day. He closed his eyes and thought about Chasity and some of the good times they had together.

Chasity sat astride him once while they were in her very large, overly soft bed. She looked down at him as she sat upon him. She dragged her well-manicured nails playfully down his chest while she started to move on top of the Gypsy. Chasity moved slowly as if he were a mechanical bull being run in *very* slow motion. He thought he saw such a routine in a movie once. He thought about "bucking" her off, and he started to chuckle a little.

Chasity looked down at him with a slightly perturbed look on her face and asked, "What's so damn funny, Blue-Eyes?"

The Gypsy laughed and thought, *I've done it again*. He responded. "I was just thinking how you look like you're riding a mechanical bull. That's all."

She leaned forward, dug her nails into his shoulders, kissed him, and said with a mischievous grin, "Don't flatter yourself." And then she started *riding* him.

The Gypsy got aroused thinking about Chasity. Chasey was *not* asleep and noticed what event had taken place. She raised her head, looked at him and asked, "What are you thinking about, Blue-Eyes?"

"Oh god. Sorry, I was just thinking about Chasity and what happened between the two of us," he replied apologetically. "I'm so—"

Chasey interrupted him with a pat on his chest, "It's all right, John. I know you weren't thinking about her in *that* way. And I don't expect you to ever forget about Chasity. She's the mother of your daughter. I know the two of you spent a lot of time together before and after we met. And I know you were close. Not as close as you are with me or Nickie, but close nonetheless."

The Gypsy calmed some, but Chasey could tell he wanted to say more, so she added, "You know, women can appear *aroused* just by getting cold or having our clothing rub against our nipples. So please don't beat yourself up over this. It's not like you were sitting in the can playing with yourself thinking about her."

He chuckled and said softly, "Thanks." After he thanked her, he gently kissed the top of her head.

Chasey lay back down, and the Gypsy tried to stop thinking about Chasity and go to sleep, but with all that had transpired today, he wound up falling asleep with memories of the two of them and the adventures they had together.

5

Chasey and the Gypsy awoke at their usual time and set about tending to the animals and morning chores. They did not wake Charity. It was summer after all, and she was in new surroundings.

"You must have been enjoying a good dream last night," Chasey commented as they finished putting the feed back and headed into the house to start breakfast.

"I don't really remember my dreams usually. Why?"

She laughed and replied, "You were moaning like a whore."

He stopped and looked down at her with that look of his. He laughed a little himself. "I dreamed about this time Chasity, and I went down by the river."

"I heard about that little adventure. You talking about when you two got caught?"

"Oh gawd! Yes" was his reply with a look of complete dejection. He stood there and shook his head as he looked at the ground.

Chasey walked back to him with a big shit-eatin' grin on her face. "What's wrong, Blue-Eyes? Did you think all your activities were unknown to everyone?"

As he laughed, he responded, "Well, I was hoping. But that was small potatoes. Chasity was a serious exhibitionist! There was this time she wanted to go swimming in the pool. I don't normally swim. I can. I just don't like to. She talked me into the pool. And well, that girl can hold her breath for a long time."

"Ya, I heard about that too. That happened after we started our little *thang*. She was sort of known for that. I probably should have said something. Sorry," she said as she grinned up at him.

"You knew she was going to do something like that and didn't say anything?"

Chasey grabbed his belt loops and pulled him in close. She reached up and brought him down so she could kiss him. After the kiss, she said "I love you" in a childish voice and promptly turned and walked back to the house. She shook her behind all the way to the house as she left the Gypsy. He stood there, shook his head and chuckled.

"I see how you are," he laughed. As he started toward the house, he added, "So that's how it's gonna be, huh? You'd better not be a bad influence on the kid!"

As Chasey entered the door to the house, she swung around and blew him a kiss.

Her father's yelling woke Charity from sleep. She staggered into the kitchen and found her parents getting breakfast ready. Charity asked, "What's all the noise?"

"Sorry, dear," replied the Gypsy. "We didn't mean to wake you. We were out doing our morning chores and were just acting up a little."

"Do you want some breakfast, sweetie?" asked Chasey.

"Sure. Do you have any Pop-Tarts?"

"We don't have anything even remotely resembling them, Charity. We don't eat processed food. With both your father's and my health issues, we have to steer clear of stuff like that."

"That's a bummer. Does that mean I don't get to eat them?"

Chasey looked at the Gypsy, and so did Charity. After he looked back and forth between the two of them, he responded, "Why are you looking at me?"

Chasey responded, "Well, *you* are her father."

He smiled and said, "Ever since I gave up sugar, processed foods, and eliminated the foods that bother me, I haven't felt this well since I was your age, honey. I'm sure I speak for Chasey when I say this, if you want them, we'll stop and get some the next time we go out. But it would be so much better for you, not only now, but for your future health, if you went ahead and got into a healthy eating habit."

While Charity thought about what he said, Chasey added, "It will be easier to do while you are young than if you wait and let your eating habits fully develop."

"It's not like we *never* have anything bad for us," the Gypsy continued. "We just eat stuff like sweets and fast food for a treat…" He paused momentarily and looked over at Chasey for confirmation and finished, "What, three or four times a month?"

"Ya. Not quite once a week. That way we appreciate the crap more," Chasey finished.

Charity stuck her bottom lip out in a pout as she looked at her father. After a slight pause, she replied, "Okay. But can we have waffles today?"

Chasey and the Gypsy laughed at Charity. They looked at each other and responded together, "Sure."

6

Chasey and the Gypsy were asleep in their bed the weekend before Charity started fall semester at her new school. Well, the Gypsy was trying to sleep. All day long, he acted like a new parent who sent their firstborn off to kindergarten. His mind ran over every detail to make sure that nothing was missed.

Did I get all the papers signed? Does she have all the supplies she needs? Wait, we didn't get any crayons, did we? He shook his head and relaxed back into his position behind Chasey. He thought, *Charity's in high school. They don't use them in high school, do they?*

He considered waking Chasey to ask her. She and Charity already chided him earlier for "losing his mind" about getting her ready for school. Instead, he settled back into his position behind Chasey and tried to relax. He thought, *If they do, we can just get them tomorrow.*

While he lay there and tried to drift off and not think about getting Charity ready for school, he started to think about Chasity again. He thought about the time he and Chasey discussed when he and Chasity were at the public pool. There were only about six or eight other people there.

He only had a pair of cutoff shorts to wear. He made them a long time ago. Chasity tried to buy him a "swimsuit," as she called it. At first she tried to get him in a thong. But that was not happening. The only other choices she gave him were all Speedos, so he just kept it old school.

Chasity, of course, had on very little. He was sure what little she did have on was very expensive. Her swimsuit had hipster-style bottoms with a Brazilian rear. It made it look as if all she had on were a belt and not much else. Plus with her long hair draped down her fit and tan back, she looked topless when viewed from behind.

Her top had three thin strings that wrapped around her neck and met as one at the top. Where they held at the breasts, there was just enough fabric to offer support and to cover her nipples, but not much else. The string that connected the two breast pieces and wrapped around the back was almost nonexistent.

Both pieces were a yellow-orange that shimmered all the different colors of the rainbow as she moved through the sun's rays. If she did not get your attention, the swimsuit made sure you noticed her. That was the only reason you wore something like that. To be noticed.

She talked (seduced) him into the pool. She needed to use beer and other ploys, but eventually they both entered the pool. As he recalled, it did not take much of either to get him in the pool. He reclined with his back against the pool edge and his arms on the ledge. Chasity faced him with her arms around his neck. She had the inside of her elbows pointed upwards toward the sky as her wrists hung down, one draped over the other behind the Gypsy's neck.

As they semifloated there and kissed, Chasity took her arms and used them to push her very expensive "store bought" breasts up under the Gypsy's chin. He remembered saying something cute, but exactly what it was escaped him. Chasity laughed. He smiled his sexy smile, and that was when she smiled her sexy smile back, and he knew he was in trouble.

Chasity pushed away slightly, took a very deep breath, and then went under. The Gypsy remembered convulsing slightly after she got down to the level of his waist. He thought his eyes were going to pop out of his head when she unbuttoned his cutoffs and slid them down to his ankles…

Chasey awoke with a slight jerk when she felt something poking her in the back. She looked back at the Gypsy with a quizzical look and asked, "Who are you thinking about tonight, Blue-Eyes?"

"Oh my god! I'm sorry. I was just trying to make sure I hadn't forgotten anything for when Charity starts school on Monday, and then I remembered what you told me before we went to bed…"

"And you didn't listen," Chasey interrupted.

"Yes! No. Not at first. Then I got to thinking about Chasity and about that time at the pool you brought up a couple of weeks ago, and one thing led to another."

Chasey rolled him over and climbed on top of him. She leaned in, kissed him gently and asked, "Do you want me to take care of it?"

"No. You don't have to. I can take care of it myself if it becomes a problem. Okay? Don't ever think that you do."

"Thank you. I want to when we get married. Just not with your daughter here."

"Ya. That would be a little weird. You being a moaner and all," he jokingly replied as he started tickling her.

Chasey squealed and slapped his hands. She held his hands above his head and said, "Stop, Blue-Eyes. We'll wake Charity."

"Oh ya, that reminds me. Do they use crayons in high school?"

Chasey burst out in laughter. She slapped her hands over her mouth as she sat atop the Gypsy and shook. She only stopped shaking when she realized he was not joking.

"Have you lost your mind, old man? How old are you? No, they don't use crayons in high school. Go to sleep."

Chasey climbed off him and lay down to try to get some sleep while the Gypsy ran through his mind to see if they had everything on Charity's school list.

7

Chasey and the Gypsy just finished getting breakfast ready and on the table when Charity staggered into the room. She yawned and scratched her backside as she plopped down at her place at the table. She wore an over-sized set of men's pajamas that she never managed to get buttoned up quite right. The Gypsy did not think her hair could possibly get any more messed up. This creature that stood before him was a far sight from what rode up the path a couple of months ago. He just shook his head and tried his best not to laugh too loudly as she plopped down at the table and rubbed the sleep from her eyes.

"Rough night on the town, sweetie?" he asked jokingly.

"Ya. What were you two weirdos doing horselaughing in the middle of the morning?"

"Oh my gawd!" the Gypsy hollered in embarrassment. He forgot all about the crayon incident. He immediately turned around to the sink and scrubbed on the plate he held in his hand. "It was nothing like that," he added as he shook his head.

"Ya. Go ahead, Blue-Eyes. Why don't you tell her?" Chasey chimed in with a little grin.

The Gypsy shot her a disapproving look and answered, "Fine!" He put his dish down and then faced his daughter and continued, "We were just discussing whether or not we had gotten all of the supplies you are going to need for the school year. That's all." He turned around and resumed washing the dish.

Charity looked as confused as ever when Chasey chimed in with, "And tell her what you asked if she was going to need." Chasey had upon her face a grin that reached from one ear to the other when she finished her comment.

"It was late, and I hadn't been to sleep. AND FYI, I STILL HAVEN'T!"

"He asked if you needed crayons."

"How old do you think I am, Daddy?"

Part V

The Black Widow

1

As Chasey and the Gypsy brought in the last of the corn from the garden, they noticed a large black car pull up their path. A very well-dressed, very dark-skinned woman was let out by her very small and timid driver. The driver was a man of small stature with milk-chocolate skin. He rushed around and let his master out of the back seat of her side of the car. As she stepped out of the car, her driver obediently looked at his feet to avoid making the mistake of looking at her.

The Gypsy dropped his handle to the bushel basket of corn, ran back into the field of corn and screamed, "No! You're supposed to be dead!"

There was only one woman that could have put that kind of fear in the Gypsy. Not even the first time he met his daughter was he able to get the strength to run. This woman was different. Chasey knew who this woman was.

She had a long fro, black as pitch that sparkled as she moved when the sun hit it. Her eyes were dark, like doll eyes, and her skin was the finest ebony. She was dressed in a full-length gown with a wide-brimmed hat. Both were emerald green and embellished with white lace. As she stepped out of her car, she opened a parasol that matched her outfit. This was a Southern lady that walked toward Chasey. Not some slutty fling the Gypsy serviced when he used to "work for a livin'," as they now called it.

The Gypsy told her about this one a long time ago. About how she left him with both physical and mental wounds that never fully healed. Chasey always wondered exactly what those *wounds* were. Now she might get the chance to find out, because before her was the Black Widow herself.

The Gypsy told her how she earned that moniker. Her first four husbands left her because of her voracious sexual appetites. Her last husband, Chasey heard through the grapevine, was thirty years her junior and fresh out of Arizona State University where he majored in being a running back on the football team. He was not good enough to go pro, but with his genetics (a Cuban immigrant mother and a father any Southern plantation owner would have been *damn* proud to have owned), this young man had the natural anatomy and endowment of which *every* man would have been jealous. Unfortunately for him, the Black Widow could spot quality, which led to his *mort d'amour*.

Charity heard her father's cry and came out to investigate. She followed the Black Widow out to where Chasey picked up the corn that spilled out of the basket. Charity kept her distance, as she went to help Chasey pick up the corn.

When the Black Widow got close enough to be heard, she said in a thick Cajun accent, "Well, it does a body to be remembered. You must be Ms. Chasey. Allow me to introduce myself, chile'. I'm Delphine Boudreaux," she said with a very warming, albeit alarming smile. She added with a slightly crooked grin, "You have probably heard stories about me under another name. I'm known as the Black Widow. A most unfortunate title to be unnecessarily bestowed upon me, I assure you, chile'."

Charity arrived next to Chasey as Delphine finished her introduction. She helped Chasey place the rest of the corn back in the basket that spilled out when her father dropped his handle.

When all the corn was back in the basket, Chasey replied, "Yes, I'm Chasey, and this is John's daughter, Charity. Would you like to join us for some tea or lemonade? Maybe Blue-Eyes will be back soon." She finished with a slight glance over her shoulder.

"That would be nice," Delphine politely replied. "I had come looking for him with the intention of talking him into coming back to Louisiana with me. But I learned he had met someone and settled down. I didn't know he had started a family."

"Well, while we are a 'family,' Charity is not my biological child."

Charity quickly interjected so Chasey would hopefully feel she was okay with the situation, which she was, "My mom frequently met with my dad, and I'm the result. I stayed with her until she passed."

Chasey looked over at Charity and smiled a soft comforting smile. As they approached the house, Chasey said to Delphine, "Your driver is welcome to join us."

"He's fine."

The Black Widow responded flatly and extremely cold, Chasey thought. *Maybe she's everything the Gypsy described. And maybe more.* She decided to give her the benefit of the doubt but still keep a wary eye on the old voodoo priestess.

She never believed in that stuff, but the Gypsy told her voodoo was nothing more than a religion.

"A little odd for a religion" was her reply, she recalled.

But the Gypsy insisted it was no different than any other. Some people took it a little extreme just like in the other more well-known religions.

As the three of them sat in the kitchen and drank their drinks, Chasey hoped Delphine left before the Gypsy got back. She could not help but wonder where he went and if he were all right.

Delphine finished spinning her tale about how she hoped to get the Gypsy to return with her. She took the last swallow from her glass and placed it back on the table. As she stood, she said, "Well, since it doesn't appear that old Blue-Eyes is going to join us anytime soon and since he has a family of his own now, anyway, I believe I shall take my leave of you."

As Delphine walked out the door, she turned to Chasey and said, "And you be sure to give Blue-Eyes my best, chile'." After she finished her command to Chasey, the Black Widow turned, moved across the porch and went to her car. She got into her car while her driver held the door like the good little puppy he was. He softly shut the door and hurried around to the other side. He hopped in the car and sped down the path in a cloud of dust.

Chasey hoped that cloud of dust was the last they saw of the Black Widow. She felt a chill go down her spine when Delphine "commanded" her to give *her* man HER best.

Chasey thought, *"Who did that bitch think she was. If she ever—"*

Charity interrupted her thought with, "Where's Dad?"

"Huh, what?" she managed as she shook the rage from her mind.

"Dad? Where did he go?" Charity asked again.

Chasey walked to the corner of the house. She jerked her thumb toward the drive and then pointed to the garden and said, "As soon as that... thing showed up, he took off into the field." Chasey turned around and, as loud as she could, screamed, "She's gone!"

2

The Gypsy stuck his head in the door as Chasey and Charity started the clean up from where they shucked and canned the corn. His two girls turned around and gave him accusing looks with raised eyebrows.

Like I had it planned, he thought as he stepped through the doorway and into the room. As he closed the door behind him, he uncomfortably started, "I... I knew if I stayed gone long enough, I would get out of doing that."

"I know that was the only reason you did," Chasey replied. She shot him a piercing stare before she and Charity turned back and continued washing the pots they used when they processed the corn they canned for winter.

"So what did she want anyway?"

"To take you back with her," Chasey said as she slammed the pan she was washing loudly into the sink so the Gypsy would know how she felt about what happened. She wanted to make sure he understood that she was not so much mad at him over that voodoo bitch as she was that he did not help with the damn corn! She stopped cleaning the dishes as the Gypsy approached and shot him a glance. He got the hint.

"You girls have done enough today. Let me finish cleaning everything up. Then I'll fix whatever you want for supper. Or we can go out."

"You're not getting off that easy, old man! You're fixing dinner, and it's going to be the messiest, most time-involved thing you know how to make!" Chasey hollered back at him from the comfort of the living room couch on which she and Charity just plopped.

"And we want a PIE for dessert too!" Charity added with a nod.

That caused Chasey to giggle. She thought, *Why did she have to nod? That was cute. Especially the way she folded her arms at the end with a little pout.*

The Gypsy heard her giggle. He started to turn to look at them with a bit of a smile on his face. Chasey decided she had better not let him think he was off the hook and snapped out, "Don't you think for one second you're out of the doghouse, old man!"

His head snapped back to where he could pay attention to the job at hand.

3

Chasey and the Gypsy were lying in bed together as they always did—she in front of him and both of them on their right sides. They always slept that way. Even after the accident and Chasey lost the hearing in her left ear, that never changed. If they needed to discuss something, they talked before they got in the bed to sleep.

Tonight sleep did not come quickly or easily for either of them, and when it finally came for the Gypsy, his dreams were not pleasant. He dreamed of the time he spent with the Black Widow. Some of the time he spent with her was fun and he had good memories. The time with Delphine was the most elegant time he spent as a male prostitute. They spent time at cotillions, fund raisers and other fancy dress parties. The experience as a whole, though, was a very dark time for him.

His dreams jumped from one experience with Delphine to another. Each one caused him more and more discomfort. She was known for her *toys*, especially early electric ones. The last dream the Gypsy had involved a particularly nasty toy that sent a capacitive charge into the device that was inserted up the…

The Gypsy bucked so violently he threw Chasey out of bed. It caused both of them to shout out.

"Oh god!" the Gypsy exclaimed as he sat bolt upright.

When he realized what happened, he hopped out of bed, pulled Chasey up, and asked, "Are you okay? I'm sorry."

"What the hell happened?" Chasey asked confused.

He took a good look at her and replied, "If that crazy bitch comes back, you have my permission to shoot first."

Chasey pulled his head into her bosom and held him close. The Gypsy looked at her after he calmed a little and added, "You don't even have to ask questions...ever."

She gently pushed him back and looked at him and asked, "Do you want to talk?"

He shook his head slightly and replied softly, "No."

"Let's try to get back to sleep, okay?"

He nodded, and they both lay down and went back to sleep. Charity, who heard the commotion while she stood outside their bedroom door, went back to bed herself and slowly went back to sleep.

4

About a month after the "infamous Black Widow incident," Chasey and Charity sat in the back of the house and shelled the last of the season's beans. The Gypsy busied himself with the breakdown of some of their latest haul to be recycled. Charity settled into her new school. Being a hot chick who rode a Harley, she was immediately very popular with everyone except the faculty. That was until the faculty found out that Charity was a very studious young lady with good parents, who just happened to ride a Harley.

They would have known the truth about her if her parents had not stopped her from leaving dressed the way she wanted to a couple of times. They did not call her Wild Cat for no reason. Now, she was not a whore. In fact, Charity was still a virgin. She had done everything else. Yes, she could hold her breath like her mother. Yet she was still a virgin, and she intended to remain one until she got married.

She tried to get out one morning with her mother's ostrich-skin boots, a pair of black fishnet stockings, and cutoff Daisy Dukes that had been bleached almost entirely white. The shorts had white lace stitched around the leg openings. The waistline was cut out and had the same lace sewn back in to line the top edge. She had a plain, ribbed, black, long-sleeve compression top for a top and a big smile on her face.

Charity remembered Chasey saw her first and said, "I don't think so, young lady."

Her father turned around as he headed toward the back door and said, "OH HELL NO!"

Charity started laughing. Chasey heard her and asked, "What are you thinking about, sweetie?"

"The time I wanted to wear my mom's outfit to school and you and Dad pitched such a fit."

"That was not appropriate for school. It was barely appropriate for a porno!"

"Yes, Mom," Charity replied most sarcastically as they both laughed. Charity got quiet and asked, "Are your parents still alive?"

"Oh, um." Chasey took a deep breath and started, "My mother died over ten years ago. She fell and broke her leg. Everything was fine. The leg was healing nicely. Mom had always been healthy. She healed quickly, went for a run, and was found dead on the side of the road. At first the police thought it was a hit-and-run, but the autopsy showed she had had a fat embolism."

"What's that?"

"Sometimes when you have a serious trauma, which during Mom's autopsy it was revealed to have been a far more severe injury to her leg than originally thought, some fat can enter the bloodstream. Sometimes it can be absorbed on its own. Sometimes it can enter the heart or brain and cause instant death."

Charity ran to Chasey and hugged her and said, "I'm sorry."

"She died instantly and felt nothing. That's the only comforting thing." Chasey smiled at Charity and then kissed her forehead. "I never got to know my father. He was in the service. Mom said he never came back. His body did, but the person who left never came home. She said he stayed for almost a year and then told her staying would be worse on everyone than going. He kissed her and told her he would never stop loving either of us. She said he told her he would send us money every month. She didn't believe him, but he did. And he still does to this day. He set up a fund with an accounting firm. It pays me or my heir."

"At least he's trying to do right."

"Ya." Chasey got quiet for a second and looked far away and then continued, "It's a little weird, but while I was out looking for *your* father, I met a man named Taylor who had helped your father. He looked a lot like what I remember my father looking like. I was in a hurry, so I didn't have time to question him about his past. I was worried about getting to your father before he did something stupid.

He had no idea I was alive. He was the only thing I could think about while I was in the hospital."

"I'm glad you found him," Charity said softly as she pushed herself up to look at Chasey.

"Me too, sweetie," Chasey replied as she brushed Charity's hair back out of her eyes.

Charity looked down and said, "I miss my mom."

"I know how you feel. I wasn't much older than you are when I lost my mom. I was just a few years out of college. Your father and I were just getting ready to leave and start our life together, and then I got hit by that truck, and not long after I got out of the hospital, Mom died. But…" Chasey paused and took a deep breath before continuing, "All that's in the past, and we have our future to look forward to now."

Charity smiled back at Chasey. She looked down and shyly asked, "Is it okay if I call you Mom?"

"Um… sure. If you're all right with it." Chasey was taken completely by surprise.

Charity nodded. Chasey said, "Okay, Mom it is."

Charity hugged her mom, and her mom hugged her back.

"What are we going to make your father fix for supper?" Chasey asked.

"Can he make a good lasagna?"

"Oh yes. That's a good one. He actually makes a good vegetarian one. Hey, John!" Chasey called out.

"What!" the Gypsy hollered back.

"How about making that veggie lasagna for supper?"

"Okay. We need to get rid of some zucchini anyway."

The Gypsy was in the kitchen fixing supper while Chasey sat in the living room and read a copy of *The Body Has a Mind of Its Own*.

Charity came in and asked, "Have you seen my backpack, Mom?

"Sorry, sweetie. I put it in the hall closet when I cleaned up."

"Thanks."

The Gypsy spun around like he was slapped. He stopped and stared at Chasey. His mouth was slightly open as he tried to comprehend what he just heard and decide on what to say.

Chasey saw him and asked, "What's wrong?"

"Did she call you Mom?" he asked softly so Charity would not hear.

"Yes, dear. We had a talk. It's fine."

"Okay," the Gypsy responded. He turned around slowly and went back to preparing supper.

5

Chasey and the Gypsy were in bed together, enjoying each other's company after a long day. They discussed the "Mom" incident as lightly and briefly as possible.

"Just try to warn me when you two plan something like that, okay? Give me a little heads-up so I can prepare. I almost lost it. I'm about to now," he added, fighting back tears.

"Okay. I'll try. Believe me. It was a real shock when she asked me. I never even expected her to even want…" Chasey's thoughts trailed off as she laid her head down on the Gypsy's chest. She continued, "You know, we still haven't set a date."

"Oh good grief!"

"I know we said we would wait until after Charity got settled. Well, she just graduated with honors from her junior year in high school while she lived with us," Chasey moved to where she sat astride the Gypsy. She placed her hands on his shoulders and stared him right in his eyes the color of the Caribbean Sea with flecks of slate and teal and said sternly, "I think she's settled."

"Okay," he answered submissively. "We'll set a date and get a place, and I'll finally make an hon—"

"Oh god, don't say that! I hate that saying," Chasey interrupted, and shook like she had a bad chill.

6

Charity was in the kitchen fixing herself a snack. She had the munchies, again. She had a little vaporizing habit she developed after a motorcycle accident. It did work great for the pain, but she mostly did it to get high now. Her knee bothered her rarely now. She just liked getting high.

She rigged herself a stealth grow under the floorboards in the closet of her bedroom. She ran the electricity from an extension cord behind her bookshelf next to the closet door and then down a whole she drilled just inside. Charity removed a section of floor and framed in a small 32" × 36" × 36" grow box complete with insulation and a lift so she could easily raise her hydroponic reservoir.

To the underside of the floorboards, she attached two 300-watt LED grow lights. She would raise the floor to provide ventilation when the lights were operating. So the light would not be seen or no one would notice anything, she only ran the lights at night when she was home. It could prove to be a little tricky, especially if the plants were in a sensitive point in their development.

She never sold anything she grew. She was not a drug dealer. She had a prescription for MMJ once, but the doctor did not renew it after she got better because she did not "need it anymore." Which was probably true, but it still did not change the fact that she still *like*d doing it. So after about a month, she went "commando" (as Charity called it) and started growing her own. She told everybody that knew she used that she got it from "some guy where she used to live."

They always believed her. But then again, everybody did. That was the one thing Charity had always disliked about her mom. The way she would always get whatever she wanted just with a wink and a smile. Everybody back home told her that her father was the same way. He could talk anybody into, or out of, anything with just a smile and a look.

She had a new mom now who seemed to be perfect. Charity stood outside her parent's room and thought about what she was doing. She listened to them discuss the fact that they still were not married. As Charity finished her chicken and pepper jack wrap with chow chow, black beans, and rice, she decided she would sleep on it and went back to bed.

7

Charity came in after she finished her morning chores. She found her father was trying to get breakfast started and her mom was working on a load of laundry.

"What's for breakfast, Pops?" Charity asked. She felt like being a real smart-ass this morning.

"Well, I was going to make some chicken fajitas omelets. But…" the Gypsy paused as he continued to dig through the refrigerator. "I can't seem to find the chicken."

"It's in the yellow lid tub," Chasey replied.

"No yellow lid tub."

"Oh!" Charity interrupted, a little embarrassed. "I had that for a snack. Sorry."

"When? I know I saw it in there last night before I went to bed!" her father asked in amazement.

"Last night. I got up in the middle of the night and wanted a snack," she replied, a little ashamed. She added a little pout for good measure.

"Oh, that's all right, sweetie. If you're hungry, get something to eat. Just as long as you're not hiding some sort of eating disorder, okay?"

"No, no," Charity responded. "No eating disorder. I was just a little hungry. That's all."

"That's fine then. I'll just make something else. Veggie omelet all right with everyone?"

"Sure," Charity and Chasey replied in unison.

Charity thought she might help Chasey with her father and in the process score some points with her. Plus, she needed a way to get the spotlight off of her, so she asked, "By the way, are the two of you married?"

"Oh, for cryin' out loud!" the Gypsy shrieked.

"I didn't say anything to her, dear," Chasey responded as the Gypsy turned to look at her.

After an awkward pause, Charity queried again, "Well?"

Being young, she could not leave well enough alone. Unfortunately, both of her parents saw her start to smile, and they realized she knew all along they were not married and that she was just trying to manipulate them.

"All right, young lady!" Chasey called out as she pulled a chair from under the table for Charity to sit. "It is not okay to manipulate people that way."

"Sorry," Charity replied as she plopped down on the chair.

"Your father and I have been together a long time and are committed to each other," Chasey held her finger up behind Charity's back to silence the smart-ass comment she could see coming from the Gypsy. Now was not the time for eighth-grade Blue-Eyes to make an appearance. Chasey continued, "We are not going to part. He had Kelly make this ring for me." Chasey held her hand so Charity could see the ring the Gypsy had had Kelly make her.

"It's beautiful. Kelly Bauer made it?"

"Yes. She doesn't just make big and bulky things. Haven't you seen her jewelry?"

"No."

"Oh goodness, yes. We'll go later if you're not doing anything. We have to take some things to the recycling center. Your father could drop us off at the smithy's and then go to the recycling center while we talk to Kelly," Chasey replied, full of excitement that she found something the two of them might have a common interest in to pursue as a hobby.

"Okay. That sounds like fun. I'm supposed to meet some friends for lunch at eleven o'clock at the Tabouret Café. What time were you thinking?" she asked with equal enthusiasm.

"You can as long as you're not planning on trying to get any beer. That's just a glorified bar. Granted they have *really* good food. But they're still just a bar," responded Chasey with skepticism.

"Ya, sweetie. Don't stay there longer than it takes you to eat, all right?" added her father.

"Okay, Dad. I will."

"We'll try to leave here around four o'clock. Then we can get some dinner somewhere and go to the grocery store after we eat."

"Sounds like a plan," the Gypsy replied.

Charity gave her "okeydoke" of approval, and everyone went back to doing their before-breakfast chores.

Part VI

Forbidden Love

1

After everyone finished breakfast and cleaned the dishes, Charity finished weeding the garden with her mom and then helped her father take apart the drill arm of some old mining machinery Chasey dragged back to recycle. She finished with the drill machine just in time to get a shower and make it to the café without having to speed.

She might have looked like it and might have even ridden something capable of it. But Charity did not like to speed.

It drew unnecessary attention to yourself and gave the pigs a reason to pull you over, she thought. She did not need to give them any reason to search her because she usually carried some of her "meds" and her vapor pipe. She would be breaking the law now that she did not have an MMJ card.

As Charity motored along on her way to meet her friends for lunch, she thought about Padric. She really wanted to have a relationship with him. She was fairly sure he was interested in her. She was unsure *how* interested he was in her. She hoped she could get him alone after lunch so she could find out just what his feelings for her were.

Charity thoroughly enjoyed the vibrations that emanated from her Harley's motor through the seat. But if she did not get to rub all over some body soon, she might hurt someone.

As the café came into view, Charity saw Padric having a loud discussion with his brother. Charity thought, *What's Padric's asshole of a brother riding him about now.*

2

Aidan Magee Mullan and Padric Magee Mullan were the fraternal twins of Hugh Mullan. Hugh was the owner and operator of the scrap-recycling center. Aidan and Padric hung out in front of the Tabouret Café with Jeff and Angie, Angie's friend Amie, and the group's weird friend Tweed (so called because he always wore a tweed vest, "just a 'cause I like it," he claimed), as they waited for Charity. The Mullan brothers were as different as night and day as their names implied.

Aidan was your stereotypical Irishman: redheaded, green-eyed, with thin chiseled features. If you threw a paddy cap and an Aran sweater on Aidan, this young man was ready for a pint. He was the mirror image of his father at this age.

But Padric was a different child altogether. He had dark hair. Not quite like the straight and black hair his mother had. His was wavy and leaned more to the brown side. He had eyes that were somewhere in between blue and green. Padric was a little taller than the rest of his family. At seventeen, he was already three inches taller than his father and a full four inches taller than his brother. He never missed a chance to remind Aidan about that fact.

Their personalities were as different as night and day as well. Aidan's temper was quick to ignite, and when he went, he could level a city block. Padric had a mild, almost-weird temperament about him. He was the type of person that you hoped you were not around when they went *pop*. He kind of reminded Charity of her father. Maybe that was what first attracted her to him when she noticed him while he worked at the recycling center for his father. He definitely would *not* have been her type if she had just met him at school. If

Charity saw him out at the mall or a restaurant, she would not give him the time of day.

But when she was there with her dad and watched Padric work with his dad, something clicked in her head, and she liked what she saw. He was the type of man she wanted. Little did Charity know that she was the type of girl Padric wanted. He was delighted to finally get his chance. Just as long as his hothead brother did not blow it for him.

"Just give... it... up," Aidan started as he taunted Padric. "A big doofus like you doesn't stand a chance at hookin' up with a *woman* like her. Her *bike* has more class than you." Aidan let out his loud screech of a laugh that always made Padric want to flatten his brother's nose.

Padric closed his eyes and thought about what his mother told him when they were little and Aidan did something similar. She patted him on his chest and told him, "Just let him go. It's not worth it." He could use one of those pats right now.

He took a deep breath and began his rebuttal, "First of all, my *bike* gets almost one hundred miles to the gallon. Granted, it's not as fast or as stylish as her *Hog*, but my 1984 Honda VT500FT Ascot 500FT is a classic masterpiece of fuel efficiency that I have modified to enhance..."

"And that's exactly why you won't score with her. She doesn't want to hear about that kind of shit," Aidan rudely interrupted.

"We'll see" was Padric's reply as Charity pulled into the parking lot. She put her bike next to Padric's and shut it down.

3

"Sup guys? I'm starved. The parents were workin' me like a rented mule," Charity started as she slapped Padric on the back and hit Aidan square in the stomach with her helmet. The hit caused Aidan to double over and gasp for air.

"DAMN! You fuckin' Amazon!" Aidan screamed when he was finally able to get some air.

"Oh, quit you whinin', ya big baby. You probably did something to deserve that and worse," Charity said. She smiled back at him as she swept Padric and Amie into the café.

After they finished their lunch, they sat at the tables and pretended they had beers to drink. When they finished their *beers*, they decided to leave the restaurant. They went outside and chatted a while. After they all told about as many lies about their bikes as they could come up with, they decided to disperse and head their separate ways until tonight.

"Want to come over and hang for a little while?" Charity asked Padric. "I have to do some things later with my mom, but we'll have a couple of hours."

"Um, sure," Padric responded shyly. He looked back to his brother who was talking to Tweed and said, "Tell Mom I'm going over to the Smiths'. I'll be home in a couple of hours."

Aidan gave him two thumbs-up with a big goofy grin with his tongue sticking out. Padric looked over at Charity. He hoped she did not see his idiotic brother's response. Luckily for Padric, he found her with a "yep, that's Aidan" look on her face as she stood there and shook her head. When Padric saw Charity's reaction to Aidan, it made him relax a little bit.

4

Charity and Padric pulled out of the café's parking lot and headed toward Charity's home. As they scooted down the road, Charity looked over at Padric and finally caught his overly cautious eye. She revved up on him and tried to get him to go faster. She was not used to all this puttering about like he did. So Charity opened her Fat Boy up and left Padric to his puttering.

He knows the way, Charity thought.

Charity stopped about midway down the drive of her home in some shade that the sun had not driven away yet and parked to wait for Padric. While she waited for him, she thought about how far she was going to let it go this time. She knew Padric now for over a year. But she was not going to lose her virginity until she was married. So that was out.

It was just their first time alone, so no need to be a ho. So no anal. She was definitely going to kiss him. Just as soon as she could figure out a good time.

But if she did not get something rubbed against her crotch soon, someone was liable to die. Their farm animals even started to look at her funny. So she was going to throw him on the ground, roll him on his back, and grind him like she was making pesto. And she did not care if her parents watched.

Maybe they'd learn something, she thought and started laughing just as Padric pulled into the drive.

Charity sat on her hog with one foot on the ground. The other leg rested on top of the tank. This seated position displayed her inner thighs in such a way that the cutoff shorts she wore rode as far as they could between her legs but were *not* in her vagina. That was the first thing Padric noticed after he brought his bike to a stop. He was no longer relaxed. He found he immediately needed to adjust his crotch. He did not get the chance because Charity came over and grabbed his shoulder. She spun him around and asked, "What kept you?"

Padric nervously kept his pelvis turned so Charity would not see his erection while he put his helmet down and started his explanation of his misperceived tardiness. "My 1984 Honda VT500FT Ascot 500FT is a classic masterpiece of fuel efficiency that I have made modifications to in order to enhance the factory efficiency of 55mpg to 65mpg to almost 100mpg."

"How?"

"I made my own cooling heat sinks for the fuel system," Padric continued. As he told Charity about all the things he did and why, Charity realized it was time.

Padric turned and looked at Charity to see if she paid attention to his explanation. He continued, "And with everything now running so much cooler..." After he finished his turn and was in the middle of his speech, she made her move.

Charity grabbed Padric by his ears and pulled him in tightly. They kissed their first kiss. As they kissed, she swept her leg behind his and wrestled him to the ground where she mounted him. As she sat atop him, she stared deeply into his eyes and started grinding her hips against his.

She started to rock atop Padric. Charity looked deeply into his eyes and started to smile. The smile was a little reminiscent of the cartoon Grinch in *How the Grinch Stole Christmas*. Padric found her smile a little unsettling, but he enjoyed himself too much to say anything at the moment.

Padric started to message Charity's breasts when a call came out from porch, "Why don't you two take that to the backyard so the neighbors won't have to watch you breed. And neither will I!" exclaimed the Gypsy.

"Daddy!"

Padric bucked Charity off and stood up. He adjusted himself and stammered, "S-s-ssoo... I'm so sorry, Mr. Smith." He followed Charity up to the porch and tried to keep as much distance between himself and the Gypsy. Padric definitely avoided making eye contact with the Gypsy.

"Relax, Paddy. I was young once. Just don't get her pregnant."

"Daddy!"

"Y-y-yes, sir, Mr. Smith," Padric replied as he still avoided eye contact with the Gypsy.

"And FYI, Daddy, I'm still a virgin," Charity replied as she acted like a big smart-ass. She followed her comment by sticking her tongue out at her father.

As Charity and Padric walked through the house, she asked him if he wanted something to drink.

"I'm good. Afternoon, Ms. Chasey," he said as Chasey entered the room from outside with the load of clothing from the morning wash.

"Hello, Padric. How are you?" asked Chasey.

"Fine, thank you."

"What was your father all up in arms about, Charity?" Chasey asked.

"He just didn't want to watch me and Padric make out, that's all."

"Wha'?" Padric said, embarrassed.

"He told us to go out back, so that's where we're going."

"Oh… well, okay, dear. You two have fun," Chasey replied, not really sure whether to believe her or not. After they went outside, Chasey set the shirt she started to fold aside and went outside to talk to the Gypsy.

"Babe, did you tell the kids to go out back and make out?"

The Gypsy laughed as he replied, "Yes." After he finished laughing, he relayed the story of what he witnessed. "They're going to do that sort of thing. I'd just as soon they do it here. Where it's safe. I just don't want to watch it, for cryin' out loud! And the neighbors shouldn't have to witness it either."

Chasey threw back her head and laughed. While she patted his back, she replied, "All right, all right. I get your point." After she finished laughing, she shook her head and went back inside to finish the laundry.

5

Padric and Charity sat behind the small barn on top of a bale of hay and rested. Padric's pants were sticky, as were most teenage boys' after they spent any amount of time in amorous activities with someone.

Charity's pants were wet as well, and she needed that. She looked at Padric as he sat there breathing hard. The sun glistened off the sweat on his forehead and cheeks. She watched one drop run down his nose. It hung on the tip until its presence annoyed him enough to cause him to huff air out of his lips to dislodge it. The exhale of air sprayed the drop into the sunlight.

As Charity watched the sweat float through the air, Padric turned to her and asked, "Are the rumors about your dad true? About what he used to do for a livin'?"

"You mean, being a male prostitute?"

"Ya."

Charity laughed and replied, "Yep. Pops was a whore and I was the result." She leaned in and kissed him and noticed how salty his lips were.

Charity pushed back. She licked her lips, looked at Padric and asked, "You ever use pot?"

"I took a hit off a joint once. You?"

"I started using it when I had a bike wreck a couple of years ago. I vape. Wanna do some?"

"Um… sure," he responded hesitantly.

"You don't have to. Don't do it just because some hot chick asks you to, okay?" she replied with a sassy attitude so he would not feel like he was pressured to do something he did not want to do.

"No, I want to. I was just making sure I did."

"Okay." Charity pulled out her vapor pipe, grinder, and small bottle of marijuana. After she ground up enough Marijuana and put it in the pipe, she let it heat up. When it started giving off vapor, she gave it a shake and handed it to Padric. She instructed, "Just inhale like a joint."

Padric did as instructed. After he inhaled the vapor, he handed the pipe back to Charity. She waited for it to generate enough vapor for her, and then she hit it. As they waited for the pipe to generate enough vapor to hit it again, the Gypsy stepped around the corner. "Hey, Charity, your mom said—That had better not be crack you're smokin', kids!" the Gypsy exclaimed when he saw what they were doing.

"No! It's just pot, Dad."

"Do you have a prescription for it?"

"Not anymore. I used to."

"All right. In the house. The both of you. Give me that," he said as he grabbed the pipe, grinder, and pot from Charity.

As the three of them entered the house, the Gypsy bellowed out to Chasey, "You'll never guess what I caught these two doing on top of a bale of hay behind the barn."

"Well, if it was worse than what you described to me that was going on in the front yard, I don't want to know. You deal with it," replied Chasey in disgust.

"Huh? No," the Gypsy chuckled a little. He held up the pipe and the other things he got from them as he continued, "They were smoking pot!"

"Well, technically, we weren't smoking pot, Dad," Charity interrupted, hoping to lighten the mood. "We were vaporizing it."

"Don't get smart."

"Sorry."

Chasey interjected to avoid a heated exchange, "Why are you using it, sweetie?"

"I started using it after I had a bike wreck. The doctor gave me a prescription for it. After I got better, he didn't renew my 'scrip. I stayed off of it for about four months. Until the first winter hit."

"I love winter. Almost as much fun as rain," her father commented sarcastically. He knew only too well of what she spoke as he turned to look out the window. That was one of the reasons he left the southeast. The humidity and rain were murder on arthritic joints and broken bones. He used that as the *reason* he left the Bayous of Louisiana. The mere thought of that area made him shiver.

"I went out and got some and have been using ever since," Charity finished, a little ashamed.

"Well, that's understandable. You do not have a prescription for it, though. You are not to be using it regardless of how you feel about it recreationally. Why? Because it does affect your memory. So please wait until you need it. There are things we can do to help with your pain. Your father wound up on heroin the same way. I don't want you to wind up that way."

"I won't," Charity blurted out.

"That's how it starts, sweetie. I'm not saying it's a 'gateway drug.' That's bullshit. But using any medications without a doctor's supervision after he has said you no longer need them is a problem," Chasey said. She hoped the explanation she gave consoled Charity.

Charity looked back and forth between her parents and the floor. She felt a little ashamed. She *liked* doing it. Especially after she got all worked up like she did with Padric. After she glanced over at Padric, who was visibly terrified, she replied simply, "I'm sorry. I'll stop"

"You've been busy all morning, Chasey. If you'll call Mrs. Mullan, I'll take these two over there. No need to bother your father at work, and I haven't gotten to meet your mother yet. Something always comes up every time we try to get together. But with eleven brothers and sisters, I don't have to tell you about that. Do I?" the Gypsy queried Padric.

"No, sir" was his response without looking up.

Chasey returned from calling Padric's mother and said, "Mrs. Mullan accepted our apologies and said to bring him on over."

"We'll be back," the Gypsy said. He grabbed the two delinquents by the arms and lead them to the Dodge where they loaded Padric's bike into the bed. The three of them got in the cab and headed to Padric's house.

As they headed down the road to Padric's, he started to mumble, "My da's gonna kill me." He started to sniffle and cry. Just a little.

He sat there with his head hung down. Charity felt bad for him. She placed her hand on his and tried to smile at him, but he would not look at her.

On their way to the Mullan's home, they passed a place where the kids hung out sometimes. Jeff, Angie, and Tweed were there with some other kids from school. The hang out spot was on a corner. In order to make the turn in the old Dodge, the Gypsy needed to slow down. Everyone was able to see them and could see Padric's emotional state. So Charity decided to help his rep and smiled her best devilish toothy grin at everyone as they passed.

She could tell it worked by the open-mouthed, wide-eyed look on Angie's face. *If I could just figure out a way to work Paddy's parents...* Charity thought.

She looked over at her father. *For an old man, he's not bad-lookin'*, she thought. She looked back over at Padric. She looked back at her father. She looked back over at Padric. Charity looked straight ahead. It just occurred to her how much they look alike in profile.

She looked back at her father and then Padric. They both have the same color eyebrows and similar-colored eyes. The eye color was a little off. Padric's were a little darker.

Huh, I guess daughters really do go for men like their fathers, she thought.

She was about to start laughing when they pulled into the Mullans' driveway. The thought of having to apologize to Padric's mother filled Charity with dread. She respected Mrs. Mullan greatly. She respected her mother as well, in spite of what she was. And she respected Chasey too. But it was different with Padric's mother. It was probably because she was more like a mother while Chasey and Charity's biological mother were more like older sisters to her than maternal figures.

After Padric and Charity unloaded his bike, they both walked up to the porch where the Gypsy waited. Padric looked at the ground as he walked passed the Gypsy. He opened the front door and walked right into his mother. He looked up and was startled when he saw her standing in front of him. He said, "Oh, hi, Mom. This is Mr. Smith."

The Gypsy stepped in the door behind Charity and spoke before he got in sight of Padric's mother, Ciara.

"I'm sorry about this, Miss…" When he saw Ciara, he knew instantly that he had met her before and from where, and then he looked at Padric. When he looked back at Ciara, the look of sheer horror on her face told him everything he needed to know. He turned to Charity as she stood between him and her brother and added, "You *cannot* date him."

"Yes, Padric, you cannot date her," echoed Mrs. Mullan.

Just as she did, Aidan walked in and asked, "Why not?"

"You, go to your room, and take your brothers and sisters to theirs, too!" ordered Mrs. Mullan. She swung at Aidan's head because he had not anticipated her order and moved quickly enough. She landed a solid smack to the back of his fiery redhead.

"Damn it! I'm going," Aidan cursed. "Come on, ya wee babbies."

"I'm just two years younger than you, you Bouzzie!" spouted back one of his siblings.

"Mom said go, and I'll still pound your arse when we get to the room," Aidan replied, chasing his brother down the hall with his fist and with the rest of his siblings in tow.

"I apologize for my children's behavior. It's their Irish blood," said Mrs. Mullan.

Turning to look at her father, Charity blurted out, "You just can't keep it in your pants, can you?"

The Gypsy licked his lips and took a deep inhale through his nose. He slowly turned his head, looked at his daughter, and said, "Apparently not, Miss Smarty-Pants."

Charity gave him a little sideways grin, and he gave her one back. She looked over at Padric, who appeared to be having a difficult time with the news. Charity wondered, *What is Padric having trouble with? The fact that the man he thought was his father wasn't, or the near-incestuous make-out session.*

We just kissed, for cryin' out loud! Charity thought.

Just as Charity was about to reach out and put her hand on Padric's shoulder, he walked over, hugged his mother, and put his head on her shoulder.

Charity said curtly, "I'll wait in the truck." She turned and left.

6

Mrs. Mullan told Padric to wait in the kitchen while the adults talked. After Padric left the room she told the Gypsy what transpired to bring them to this day since they met at her college friend's bachelorette party almost eighteen years ago.

"Hugh told me the story of you and Chasey. When I saw you at the grocers once, I knew it was you. Every time Hugh tried to invite you over, I came up with an excuse to avoid you."

She told him about being ashamed when she got out of control at the party and joined in the orgy. She told him how when she arrived home she made love to Hugh. It was more of a way to make herself feel better than anything else at first. Since then, everything she did was to make it up to him.

"Stop punishing yourself so much. I'll keep your secret and make sure Charity and Chasey do until you have time to tell Hugh and the rest of the family," the Gypsy said. He tried to be as consoling as he could. "Um, if… when Padric's ready to talk to me, tell him to come on over and see me. Okay?"

"Okay. I'll tell Hugh tonight. I'm sure he's always known. The only way there would have been any more obvious sign of my infidelity would have been if he was born with darker skin," Ciara said. She took a deep breath and exhaled heavily. She smiled for the first time since the Gypsy walked into her home.

The Gypsy smiled back and said, "Just let me know if there's anything I can do."

Ciara smiled and nodded. The Gypsy threw up his hand as he walked out the door. As he walked down the path to the truck,

Charity watched her father intensely. The Gypsy saw that look before, so he never bothered to look at her.

He walked around the truck, got in, and hit the starter. For the first time since he was with Chasey, the truck failed to start on the first try. The Gypsy sat there for a second and sucked some air through his front teeth as Charity forcefully blew a lungful of air out of her nose.

The Gypsy turned the key off and back on. He hit the starter again. *Vroom!* He clicked his teeth and pulled out onto the street. As they went down the street, he tried not to notice his daughter as she stared a hole in his head.

As they got to Charity's hangout corner, she stopped looking at her father and looked down at the floor of the truck.

As they slowed to make the turn, Angie called out, "Hey, Chair, you comin' back out later?"

The Gypsy answered for her, "Charity won't be around for a while. She and Padric got in trouble smoking pot." He threw up his hand at the kids as he made the turn and headed toward home.

Charity kept her head down for the remainder of the trip home. When they arrived home, they walked up to the house in silence. As they walked through the front door, the Gypsy said, "Why don't you fire that thing up one last time. I think we both need to smoke some right now before I have you throw it all out."

"Good!" Charity exclaimed.

"Now, wait one minute. Just what happened over there?" Chasey asked with a concerned tone.

"Ya, Pops, why don't you tell her what happened *over there* while I get this ready," Charity said with as much of an attitude as she could. "It'll be good for you. You know the old sayin', 'The truth will set you free.'"

"Now, young lady, I didn't have to be nice and let you have one last hit. But let's not forget the fact that *you're* the one in trouble here, not *me*." And without missing a beat, he turned to stare Chasey right in her eyes and added, "And Padric's my son."

You would have thought a truck hit Chasey again. The silence was almost maddening. The only movement in the house was

Charity's head as it nodded confirmation while she readied the vaporizer. Chasey looked over at Charity when she handed her the vaporizer. Chasey took it, breathed in its vapor and then handed it back to Charity.

7

Chasey, Charity, and the Gypsy sat around the kitchen table after they brought Chasey up to speed on everything that transpired during the time they were away. Charity would mention her concerns about Padric's reaction later. As they sat there and enjoyed Charity's "meds," they contemplated the implications of what happened. The Gypsy snapped out of his trance and was the first to speak.

"Would the person you got this weed from be willing to buy it back? It seems a waste to throw it out if there's much of it left."

Charity cut her eyes over to her father and said, "I only bought my first bag." She switched her look over to her mother and continued, "Three years ago..."

"Wait, what?"

"Just where *are* you growing it, dear?" Chasey asked.

Charity placed her hands on the table and slowly pushed herself up. As she walked toward her room, she motioned for them to follow with a sweep of her arm.

"Wait... what?" the Gypsy queried again.

As they entered Charity's room, she approached her closet and slowly slid the door open. She stood there with a flat grin on her face as her parents gave her an "I don't see anything" look. Charity pushed back her clothing. She raised the section of floor that had the lights attached and hooked it in place. She got the hoist out and attached it to the hook mount she had in the ceiling and raised her hydroponic grow chamber that contained three plants of varying heights.

"Ta-da!" Charity exclaimed with pride.

Her parents looked at her in total amazement.

"Okay," her father started. "Aside from the fact that everything you're doing is completely and totally illegal," he paused as he looked her setup over. After he completed his inspection, he continued, "this is amazing work, sweetie. You even insulated. Was that to avoid detection, or to keep the weather out?"

"A little of both," Charity replied. She beamed with pride at what her father said.

Chasey chimed in with, "Well, the pot has to go, but we can set up the hydroponic system and grow veggies over winter."

"Yep," the Gypsy agreed.

"Bummer."

8

Things calmed down around the Smith household, and Charity served out the remainder of her sentence without incident. No one in the family heard anything from Padric, but they heard from Ciara and Hugh a few times.

The Mullans put Padric into counseling. He started having nightmares the first night. Or at least that was what he told everyone. He kept having the same dream or variations of it. He was with Charity, and they did way more than kiss.

Charity would wind up pregnant in all his dreams, but after that, all the dreams changed. Some were weird. She would give birth to monsters and bizarre creatures. But in some, she gave birth to a normal child and they lived happily ever after.

That's the one that bothered him. He was all right with the monster and the weird. But the happily ever after bothered him. He hoped he would be able to get everything worked out before school started back. It was going to be close.

After some brief counseling, Padric finally started to sleep through the night. He still had the dreams, but they became fewer and less severe. Some of them became comical. Still sexual in nature, but comical nonetheless. His most recent one involved him and Charity nude atop a tiny teeter-totter. They held hands and wore their motorcycle helmets.

I can't wait to find out what the doctor has to say about this one, he thought as he wrote it in his journal before he turned out his light and went back to sleep.

Chasey and the Gypsy both spoke with Hugh Mullan.

He said, "Everyone had a suspicion. I knew something was up the day she came back from that bachelorette party. The night after, she made me the best meal I had ever had. And well, I'd rather not say any more. But Ciara more than made up for any indiscretion she might have had that one night. She has given me eleven wonderful children, including Padric. Well, we'll call it ten and Aidan. Ain't that right, Daddy's little Bouzzie?" Hugh hollered out to Aidan, who was propped up reading a magazine of some ill repute.

Aidan only looked up long enough to spit.

"If Padric ever wants to come over and talk, he is more than welcome. He's even welcome to stay anytime he wants," said the Gypsy.

"Yes, anytime," echoed Chasey.

"Tell Ciara hello for us, and we'll get out of your hair, Hugh."

"I will."

They all shook hands, and Chasey and the Gypsy left the recycling center and headed home to Charity.

9

The Gypsy and Chasey arrived back home and stored the trailer in its place. The Gypsy went around back to check on the animals and grab some eggs to use for supper. Chasey went inside to find Charity to let her know they were home and to update her on what became known around the house as "the Padric Affair."

"Charity?" Chasey queried.

"I'm cleaning the bathroom, Mom," Charity called out from down the short hall.

Chasey poked her head into the bath and said, "Hey, we had a good talk with Mr. Mullan. He said he had suspected something the very night Mrs. Mullan came home. Evidently, she's been so torn with guilt she's been trying to make amends ever since. But now that it's out, she has relaxed, and he said it has been good for their 'life.'"

"What do you mean?"

"It made everything in their life better. Every aspect because Ciara is no longer guilt-ridden about what happened with your father. Hugh said he suspected all along but forgave her."

"Oh. Well, good. How's Paddy?"

"He's doing better. He's able to sleep through the night now. But Mr. Mullan said the therapist told him there's something Padric's afraid to talk about."

"Well, a blind person can see what that is!" Charity blurted out.

"Honey, not everybody was raised in as, how shall I say, 'morally loose' an environment as were you."

Charity stuck her tongue out at Chasey and replied, "I know. I'm still attracted to him. *But* I don't want to have sex with him anymore. Eww! But he's still the same person that I wanted to be with and was attracted to in the first place. He was my *best* friend. *Is*."

"Give him time. He also didn't have someone with a degree in psychology living with him for the past couple of years."

"Ya, that couldn't hurt."

The Gypsy came in as Charity and Chasey hugged. "You guys mind taking that someplace else? I need to use this."

Charity looked up at him from the seated position she and Chasey were in on the edge of the tub and commanded, "I'm cleaning the bathroom! You'll just have to use the bushes!"

Chasey gave him a haughty look of "I guess she told you."

"Fine!" he shot back. "Why is it, she's the one who's grounded, yet I'm the one who always gets punished?" the Gypsy ranted as he went out back to facilitate. After the door closed, Charity and Chasey could hear the Gypsy exclaim, "Could someone please explain it to me!"

10

As they finished dinner, Charity looked up from her plate. She looked right at her father with as much mischievousness as she could express in her doll-like face, and said, "You know, Chasey, it's just a couple of weeks 'til school. We've got time to plan your wedding."

"Wha'? Why?" the Gypsy exclaimed as he slammed his hands down on the table. "What did I ever do to you? I brought you into this world and…"

As Charity and Chasey mocked the Gypsy and emphasized what they said with a thrust of their fists into the air, the three of them in unison finished, "I can take you out!"

The Gypsy grunted his disapproval of their involvement.

"Now, about this aversion you have to getting married…" Chasey started.

"Now, don't you start your shrinky dinkin' on me, young'un," the Gypsy interrupted. He pointed his fork at her while he looked at her with one eye.

Chasey crinkled her nose at him and said, "Finish your quiche, which, by the way, is perfect."

"I know. And you ruined it. It was the best one I ever made, and I'll probably never make another its equal," he said. He started acting like he was crying. He pouted and sniffled as he finished. He sat and stared at his plate as he flicked the remaining food with his fork like a child.

He made a fake sniffle and wiped away nonexistent tears and snot with his arm. Chasey watched his display grow more juvenile until she could take no more. "You'd better put a stop to those 'crocodile tears' right now, old man."

He fought as best as he could to resist smiling, but it was to no avail. Chasey caught him, and then he started laughing.

"You're too weird, Dad," Charity commented.

"John, seriously, what's up with you and us finally getting married?" Chasey begged.

The Gypsy chuckled. "Oh, nothing. I'm just one of those 'If it ain't broke, don't fix it' kind of people. That's all." He reached out and patted the hand she placed on the table and added, "You two go ahead and plan your wedding. Just leave me out of as much of it as possible."

"Okay, what size dress are you?" Chasey asked in jest.

The Gypsy stopped almost to the sink. He turned, placed one hand on his hip and gave her a look—the one everybody has with a raised eyebrow and sternly pursed lips—while he looked down his nose at her. He stuck his tongue out at her, and they both chuckled.

"And you two *don't* do drugs? Maybe you should start," Charity suggested.

Chasey reached over, grabbed Charity's hand, and shook it lovingly. She got up to get a notebook to start planning her wedding. As she went to the desk, she asked, "Where do you want to have it, John? You know so many people from all over the place."

"Well, the only people I care about are within a couple of hundred miles of here. I know a lot of people in the Vegas area. That's not too far from here or the town you grew up in. There are a couple of really nice places between here and Vegas too."

"And a whole lot of really great places," Chasey added as she walked up to the Gypsy. She pulled him down, placed her arms around his neck, and kissed him. As she did, he picked her up, and she wrapped her legs around him. It caused him to sit back against the counter a little hard, which caused the dishes to rattle.

The two of them started breathing heavy and lightly moaning together on the counter. Charity, not impressed with the show they were putting on for her, shouted out, "Is that the best you can do? Or do I need to go get my brother and show you how it's done? Take it out in the backyard so I don't have to watch it!"

Chasey turned to Charity, and apologized, "Sorry, dear. I'm just happy we're finally going to get married." She turned right back to the Gypsy and checked, "We are getting married, right?"

"Yes. As soon as you get everything set, we'll do it. We'll go tomorrow and get the license."

"Tomorrow's Sunday."

"We'll go MONDAY and get the license, okay?"

"Okay," Chasey agreed. She kissed him one final time and climbed down. She was giddy like a little schoolgirl as she went back to the table with Charity where they started planning the wedding.

11

It was almost a week since the Gypsy made his confirmation to Chasey that he really would marry her. All they had to do was get the date set and plan it. She and Charity worked tirelessly as they planned it. When they were not working on breaking something down to take to the recycling center or taking care of the garden and animals, they planned the wedding.

"You've got so many magazines and books in the house it's beginning to look like a wedding planner's office exploded in here," the Gypsy commented with a grin.

Charity and Chasey responded in stereo by sticking their tongues out at him.

"Oh, before I forget, Blue-Eyes. You need to get your tux. This week, please!" Chasey smiled a big toothy grin with her eyes tightly closed. The Gypsy gently grabbed her nose and gave it a little shake as he passed her. "I mean it!" she called out to him as he went down the hall.

"Yes, dear," floated back up the hall.

"Is Dad going to get his tux?" Charity asked softly, concerned he might be trying to get out of getting married.

"Yes. He's just going to make me suffer just because he doesn't *want* to get married. That's all."

Charity's eyes got wide. She grabbed Chasey by the arm and said, "Dad."

"What?"

"Your dad. We have to find him. Do you remember where you met him?"

"I'm not even sure it *was* him."

"If who was him?" the Gypsy asked as he walked back into the room.

"Sit down, babe," Chasey requested. "I never got around to telling you about this. Not quite sure how to start."

"This had better not be about ANOTHER child of mine!" the Gypsy exclaimed as he shot up out of his chair after he just sat down.

"No! No!" Chasey said as Charity sat and shook her head at her father. "While I was looking for you after..." Chasey paused and looked over at Charity before she continued, "I got hit by the truck." Chasey took a deep breath and finished, "I met a man who I think might have been my father."

The Gypsy's jaw dropped.

Chasey told him about when she met a man named Taylor. She told the Gypsy that Taylor told her he knew the Gypsy and put her on a possible path to find him.

"If I had only had enough time to stay and ask him about who he was. But I had to find you."

"I spent some time with a man named Taylor. We have to go and see if he's still there. If he is your father, he should have the opportunity to give you away at your wedding," the Gypsy added. He was amazed at how she followed him.

"And I can find out," Chasey added.

"And there's that too," he concluded, taking her chin in his hand.

12

School started for Charity and Chasey made her plans to go find out if Taylor was her father. The Gypsy surprised everyone. He went out and got his tuxedo the very next day after Chasey asked him. He impressed them with his choice of style. It was from the Regency period. The black coat was cut high in front with long tails. It was paired with a maroon paisley waistcoat. The black top hat's silk band, the coat pocket silk, and cuff links all matched the waistcoat. The pants were black with a Navy pinstripe. And on his feet, a pair of maroon elephant skin cowboy boots.

Charity shook her head as she thought about how her mom got on to him about wearing boots with the suit.

Her father replied rather snootily, "Not everybody can afford Hugo Boss, my dear lady!" In which a rather nasty argument ensued about the cost of his boots and the death of the elephant, blah, blah, blah. Charity remembered she was riding her bike to school just in time to see the curve. She managed to slow down enough and get the bike under control to safely make the turn. She took a deep breath and sat up a little taller for the rest of the ride in to school.

When Charity arrived at school, she was pleased to see Padric's bike parked next to Aidan's. *At least he's here*, she thought.

Angie came running up just as Charity shut down her Harley and asked, "Hey, Chair! Where you been? Ain't seen you last part o' summer."

"Ya, Paddy and I got caught vapin' pot, and I got it pretty bad," Charity replied dejectedly. She added excitedly, "Then I got all tangled up in helpin' Mom get her wedding planned. They're finally gonna do it!"

After Charity got off her bike, the girls grabbed hands and screamed like schoolgirls. Charity grabbed her books, gloves, and helmet. As they staggered up the path to the school building, she threw her arm around Angie.

Charity bid good morning to Angie after they arrived at her locker. She put her helmet, gloves, and the books she would not need immediately inside and shut the door. After she locked the door, she turned to see Padric at his locker. She was unsure if she should speak to him, but if they did not speak, everybody would know something was up.

So Charity walked up and asked, "Is it all right if we talk, Paddy?"

Padric shut the door to his locker. He took a deep breath, looked at her for the first time since he found out they were brother and sister, and smiled at her. He looked down, while he tried to maintain the appearance that he was looking at her, and said, "Yes. I'm okay now. I was just having some really weird dreams."

"Can't you look at me?"

He closed his eyes, took another deep breath, and looked at her. He looked away and answered, "Not yet."

"Can we talk about it?"

Padric laughed, "HELL NO! Not now and maybe not EVER."

Charity smiled and giggled a little. She placed her hand on his shoulder. When he did not recoil, she knew he would be all right. She kissed him on his cheek and, as they approached his class, she said, "See you next period."

Padric found he was unable to stop himself from saying what came out of his mouth next, "Later, sis."

The events that transpired after he said "Later, sis" went down in history as "the day time stopped" at their high school that morning.

13

It was not bad enough that he called her "sis" in school. It was not even that bad that he did it in front of some of their friends. It was not even that bad that he said it in front of the school guidance counselor, who just happened to be getting a visit from his therapist. No, that was nothing. At the very moment he said "Later, sis," that redheaded asshole of a brother of his walked up right in front of him.

Aidan stopped and said in a very loud and boisterous voice, "What? Is that why Mom and Mr. Smith said you couldn't shag this scrubber?" He fell down on the floor, grabbed his sides, and began to horselaugh.

Padric took a step toward Aidan but was grabbed by his therapist, who said, "Why don't we go talk," as he escorted Padric away.

Angie, two other girls and two teachers, one male and one female, tried to restrain Charity. The school counselor grabbed a still-laughing and in-complete-tears Aidan by the ear. He pulled him up and said, "And you come with me, young man. Let's see if I can't teach you the meaning of the word *tact*."

The counselor led Aidan around the corner and down the hall. While she still shook with anger, Charity said, "You can let go."

Everyone released Charity and stepped away from her. She collected herself, took a deep breath, and said, "Yes. Padric's my brother. My father was a male prostitute. At least eighteen years ago.." she paused. She made strong hand gestures in the direction Padric and his therapist exited and continued, "Somehow this…"—she paused briefly to collect herself—"happened. Everybody knows. It's all water under the bridge, as they say. Padric's had a little bit of a rough time because of…" Charity went into a fit as she pointed in the direction

Aidan was hauled off. Her fit included a few single-finger waves as she finished her tirade with, "THAT!" After she took another deep breath, she continued, "So Paddy needs our help and understanding, okay?"

Everyone smiled and nodded. Some even verbally ended with an "okay" or "sure." The teachers started herding the children to their rooms as the bell rang for classes to start.

14

After Charity arrived home from school, she walked around the house in search of Chasey. She found her working on their small tractor. When Chasey saw Charity, she said, "I got a call from the school today." She laughed and added, "I'm sorry."

"It's not funny, Mom."

"I know. Doesn't Aidan know you would have killed him? One day there's not going to be people around to save him."

"Paddy was about to jump him," Charity said with genuine concern.

"Oh, so I see. It's that bad."

"Yes. I'm pretty sure if his therapist hadn't been there, Paddy would have killed him."

"He was standing up for the honor of his sister after all," Chasey said, smiling softly. "But I'm not sure he would have killed him."

"Mom, Aidan torments Padric. I was a little worried about him before this. Now I'm really concerned."

At that moment, Chasey remembered the missed signs and chances she had to help Michael before he killed himself.

"You're right, sweetie. Let's talk to your father. We'll see if we can add on another room and have Padric stay here if he wants to."

Charity beamed. "Oh, Mom! That would be wonderful."

The Gypsy walked up with a couple of glasses of water for Chasey and himself and heard his daughter's exclamation. He asked, "What would be wonderful?"

Charity looked at Chasey for permission, and her mother motioned for her to explain. She told her father of Padric's situation and asked, "If he would be all right with it, could we add on to the house and let him stay here?"

"Are you onboard with this?" he asked of Chasey.

"Sure. We'll be able to manage. We have enough in savings for a small master addition."

"What's Paddy think about it?" the Gypsy asked.

"Can I go over and ask him, Dad? That would probably be better."

"We should all go, dear. I'll call Mrs. Mullan and make sure they're going to be there and tell her what's up and see what she thinks," suggested Chasey.

"That's probably a good idea," agreed the Gypsy.

While Chasey went inside and called Ciara, Charity leaned against the tractor tire and worried about Padric. The Gypsy could tell she was upset. When she looked up at him, the only thing he could think to do was to stick out his tongue at her. Charity tilted her head like a dog that heard something strange and stuck her tongue out at him.

The Gypsy smiled at his daughter, and she smiled back. "So is this how it's gonna be with your brother too?" he asked.

"Probably."

"Good. I wouldn't have it any other way."

Chasey walked back out and announced, "I talked to Ciara, and she said she thought that would be a good idea."

Charity squealed.

Chasey continued, "She said Aidan and Padric had been at each other ever since they got home. She would talk to Hugh and Padric while we head that way."

15

Hugh took Padric out back to the woodshed. He never had to take him out there before. This was a familiar trek he made many times with Aidan. And one he made with his own father many times as well. But this was the first time he came out here with Padric, and it was not for a beating. Mr. Mullan was fairly sure he stopped being able to beat Padric a couple of years ago.

Hugh took Padric out there to talk with him. A very serious talk with him. Ciara told him what the plan was, and Hugh agreed it would be best for everyone involved as long as Padric was agreeable. That was why they were out there.

"Son, I want you to know how proud I am of you with how you handled yourself with Aidan. I know I couldn't have done it. It's all I can do to keep from pounding his arse every day," Hugh said. He tried to laugh as much as he could while he placed his arm around Padric.

"Thanks, Dad. I don't know how much more of him I can take," Padric said. He looked down at his hands as they slowly stopped shaking.

Ciara walked up behind them and asked, "Have ya asked him yet, *mo mhuirnín dílis?*"

"Not yet, *mo stoirín.*"

"Asked him what?" Padric asked with a little concern.

Ciara told Padric of the Smith's idea and then asked, "If you would be wi—"

"Yes!" Padric answered before Ciara was able to finish asking. "I'm sorry," Padric apologized. "I've just had all I can take of Aidan."

"We understand," Ciara said as she tried to comfort him. She continued, "They're here waiting for you."

ARTOOLLIOUS

Padric's eyes got wide with excitement. He started to cry but got himself together. He swallowed hard, nodded and said, "Okay, I'm ready."

16

Charity and Padric rode home in the back of the old Dodge arm in arm. Charity could not stop smiling.

Padric finally had all of her attention he could take and asked, "What's up with you?"

"I'm just glad we're going to get to be together, Paddy. I missed you." Charity laid her head on his shoulder and added, "And I love you." She looked back at him for his reaction.

"And I love you. I just hope those weird dreams don't mess me up." He quickly added, "Like my sister! Ya know."

They both laughed and smiled. Charity replied, "I know," as she laid her head back on his shoulder.

"Just a little warning," Charity continued as she sat up and looked at Padric. "Dad's nuts, and Mom's not far behind him. But she does have a degree in psychology, so don't be afraid to talk to her, 'kay?"

"Okay," Padric answered as they pulled into the drive of their house.

"All right, Family Smith, let's get Padric's things inside and find a place for everything. The two of you still have school tomorrow," the Gypsy said after he got out of the truck.

Chasey followed and added, "We can stack the boxes in the kitchen between the doors where we keep the shoes. I'll move them when we get in."

As they moved Padric's things in, the Gypsy commented, "Paddy, you can sleep on the couch, unless..." He let his comment drift off as he looked in Charity's direction when she walked past him.

"John!" berated Chasey.

"Daddy!" complained Charity.

Padric stood there with a complete look of shock on his face.

"No! No!" the Gypsy shouted as he waved his arms back and forth. "I was just motioning to the hammock. It's still nice enough he could sleep outside," he managed to add with a look of complete innocence.

"You're full of shit, old man!" yelled Chasey as she pointed at him. That caused the Gypsy to start laughing.

"Just for that, Padric can have our room and you can sleep in the hammock!" Chasey chastised the Gypsy.

"Wait, what?" was all the Gypsy managed to say.

"Told ya. Nuts," Charity said as she walked past Padric on her way to get another load of his things.

Charity thought for a second and added, "I may have screwed you without us ever having to take our clothing off." She turned and vanished outside to the truck.

Padric hollered out after her, "You're as nuts as they are!"

The Gypsy chimed in with "Welcome to the family, son!" as he walked toward him with his arms wide and a big goofy smile on his face.

17

The Smiths got the addition under roof and were going to put the shingles down over the weekend. The Gypsy spent several nights on the hammock. Chasey finally allowed him to sleep on the floor for one night before she let him get in the sleeper sofa with her.

As they finished up their early breakfast, Chasey looked over at the Gypsy and said, "Well, Blue-Eyes, you managed to postpone getting married, AGAIN!"

Charity staggered around the corner. When she heard Chasey's comment, she asked, "What? Oh my god, Dad! You probably planned all of this, didn't you? You probably even planned on having us." Charity pointed frantically back and forth between her and Padric as he ate his breakfast.

"Huh? Wha'? Leave me out of this," Padric mumbled as he shoveled more cereal into his mouth.

Charity continued her rant, "No, no, think about it. He knew one day he would get saddled by some little cuttie that would try to tie him down."

"He doesn't like being tied down," Chasey interrupted. "Now, tied up... that's a story for another day," Chasey finished as she looked over at the Gypsy seductively.

"Eww," replied Charity flatly.

Padric stopped midraise of his spoon and looked over at Chasey and then at his father. He placed his spoon back in his bowl and pushed it away. He sat back in his chair, held his stomach and moaned, "Gag."

"Sometimes," the Gypsy replied thoughtfully.

Padric pretend-retched and ran to the sink.

Charity said, "Gross, wha'? No. Check it. It would be easy for him to conveniently 'forget' to wear a condom. Or maybe poke a hole in some," Charity mimicked poking something.

"One of the benefits of being a heroin addict was I always had needles with me," the Gypsy confirmed.

"See, Mom, he admits it," Charity said while she laughed and pointed an accusative finger at her father.

"Are we going to have to go to the Justice of the Peace and have him marry us just so you all will believe me?" the Gypsy queried.

Chasey halted the suggestion with, "No! I do not want to get married that way. I want to get married in a church. I can wait, okay?"

"All right then. Will you two cut out the conspiracy-theory crap? Please?" he said with an added cheesy grin on *please*.

Chasey and Charity agreed in unison with "Okay."

"You finished with your breakfast, boy?" the Gypsy asked of Padric.

"Ya, let me get it," Padric grabbed his dish, drank the remaining cereal and placed his bowl in the sink. He turned to face his father and asked, "We ready to put the shingles on?"

"The Mullans will be here in just a minute. But we can go ahead and get everything ready," the Gypsy replied as he stood.

The Mullans helped with the addition as much as the could. Even Aidan helped out. Padric's and Aidan's relationship was much better since Padric moved in with the Smiths. They spoke more as friends and not as competitors, which was what everyone was in agreement on as being their main point of conflict.

After Padric moved out, Aidan started helping out at the recycling center. His father did not have to ask more than one hundred times like before. Hugh even bragged on Aidan now. He never used to do that. Good things can come out of bad situations sometimes.

"While the two of you get ready for that, Charity and I will take care of the animals before everybody gets here," suggested Chasey.

"Sounds like a plan," responded the Gypsy.

FIN

One ring, two rings. *Click.* "Hello?"

"Oh, uh, this is Nickie. Is Chasey there?"

"Hey, Nickie! It's Charity. She's in the addition with Dad. I'll go get her."

"Thanks," Nickie replied flatly.

"What's up, Nickie?" Chasey asked.

"I need your help."

About the Author

After being hit by a car while cycling and winding up on disability, the author sat at his desk trying to come up with a way to get back to some form of gainful employment. He had written poetry and prose before the accident that put him on disability but never had the time for novels. He had many ideas for novels that were complete in his head but was never able to get anything down on paper after his accident.

One day while banging his head on his desk while trying to write, he thought, *What am I ever going to be able to do if I cannot do something as seemingly facile as writing? Well, there's always the oldest profession.* Even if he had been willing to prostitute himself, his injuries would have prevented him from preforming such activities. Then a light bulb went off, and *The Gypsy Chronicles* was born and flowed freely onto the computer, breaking whatever block had been there, allowing him to be able to write all the books and plays he had floating around in his brain.

CPSIA information can be obtained
at www.ICGtesting.com
Printed in the USA
LVHW042336180919
631539LV00001B/12